FOR 82 YEARS, THE UNIQUE MAGAZINE

December 2004

ISSN 0898–5073

Cover by Tom Kidd

Weird Tales® is published 6 times a year by DNA Publications, Inc., & Wildside Press, LLC in association with Terminus Publishing Co., Inc. Postmaster and others: send all changes of address and other subscription matters to DNA Publications, Inc., PO Box 2988, Radford VA 24143–2988. Single copies, $5.95 in U.S.A. & possessions; $7.00 by mail to Canada, $10.00 by first class mail elsewhere. Subscriptions: 6 issues $24.00 in U.S.A. & possessions; 33.00 in Canada, in U.S. funds. Editorial matters and single-copy orders should be addressed to *Weird Tales*®, 123 Crooked Lane, King of Prussia PA 19406–2570. Publisher is not responsible for loss of manuscripts in publisher's hands or in transit; please see page 8 for more details. Copyright © 2004 by Terminus Publishing Co., Inc. All rights reserved; reproduction prohibited without prior permission. Typeset & printed in the United States of America. *Weird Tales*® is a registered trademark owned by Weird Tales, Limited.

Cold Tonnage Books, 22 Kings Lane, Windlesham, Surrey, GU20 6JQ, United Kingdom, andy@coldtonnage.co.uk, offers subscriptions to *Weird Tales*® at £27 for six issues in the United Kingdom, £30 elsewhere, payment in sterling by cheques, money orders, or Pay Pal.

PURE PULP FICTION!

The Maker of Gargoyles, by Clark Ashton Smith
600-copy hardcover edition, $29.95.

Clark Ashton Smith was a prodigy who wrote Arabian Nights novels in his mid teens and was heralded as a major voice in American poetry by the time he was nineteen. In one frantic burst in the middle 1930s, he wrote nearly a hundred strange, wondrous, and grotesque stories, most of which were published in *Weird Tales*, *Strange Tales*, *Wonder Stories*, and other pulps, but he was by no means a conventional pulp writer. A direct heir to Edgar Allan Poe and to the late Romantics and Decadents, Smith wrote in baroque, jeweled prose of distant times and remote planets, of baleful magics and reanimated corpses, lost lovers, eldritch gods, and inexorable fate.

Think of him as the sorcerer-poet, alone in his eyrie in the dry California hills, dreaming his strange dreams and creating his unique worlds—of Zothique, the Earth's haunted last continent at the end of time; Hyperborea, a prehistoric land; Poseidonis, the last foundering isle of Atlantis; and Averoigne, an unhistoried province of medieval France, thick with vampires. Think of the visions his stories conjure up as sendings, written in strange runes, transported from the sorcerer's lair by indescribable genii or winged spirits.

This fine collection of Clark Ashton Smith's work reprints eight of his classic fantasies, including two set in Hyperborea.

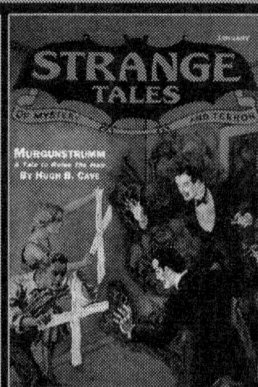

OUT OF THE WRECK	SATAN'S DAUGHTER	FAR BELOW	THE BLACK MASK	STRANGE TALES
by Capt. A.E. Dingle	by E. Hoffmann Price	Ed. by Robert Weinberg	(May 1922 - 2nd issue!)	(Jan. 1933 - 7th issue!)
$14.99 (trade pb)	$15.95 (trade pb)	$15.95 (trade pb)	$19.95 (trade pb)	$19.95 (trade pb)
	$40.00 (hardcover)	$35.00 (hardcover)		

Where Have We Been?

Yes, it's been entirely too long since our preceding issue. Briefly, we changed distributors, not once, but twice. We greatly underestimated the disruption this would cause, not only to getting on the newsstands and into bookstores, but also to our schedule. We hope to have significantly improved distribution in the future.

What Does a Story "Mean"?

We recently came across an article in that classic reference work, *Uncle John's Bathroom Reader* (compiled by the Bathroom Readers' Institute, and published by St. Martin's Press in 1988), which outlines the more or less absurd theory that L. Frank Baum's *The Wonderful Wizard of Oz* is "really" a political allegory about late 19th century Populism, the gold standard, and William Jennings Bryan, who appears in the book as the Cowardly Lion, all oratorical roar and nothing else. Allegedly, when Bryan's run for the US presidency in 1896 failed, Baum was inspired to write the book. Bryan felt that the little people (Munchkins) were being oppressed by the gold standard and that all would be well if the country shifted to a silver standard, which would make money plentiful. Dorothy's house kills the Wicked Witch of the East (eastern bankers), frees the Munchkins, and then she and her companions depart on the Yellow Brick Road (gold standard) to the Emerald City (Washington) where she confronts the Wizard (president), who is a humbug who hides behind a false image.

To which most readers today, particularly the younger ones, might say, *"Huh?"*

But wait, there's more. How about this? One of the pseudopods of *Weird Tales*®'s amorphous Editorial Horde (Darrell) was on a panel at Capclave last Fall called "Twisted Tolkien," which was devoted to new and different interpretations of *The Lord of the Rings*. For instance, we put on our Commie Hat (a Chinese "Mao cap" with a red star in the appropriate place — actually a Soviet cub scouts pin, with a flaming profile bust of Lenin in the middle) and begin as follows, assuming a fake Russian accent:

"Comrades! Clearly *The Lord of the Rings* glorifies the revolt of the oppressed masses against the snivelling bourgeois hobbits and disgusting Gondorian and Elvish running-dog lackeys of decadent divine-right monarchy. The heroic Orcs, representing the working class, struggle for freedom, but all ends in tragedy because Samwise, a downtrodden proletarian if ever there was one, fails to understand the need to push Frodo into the fiery pit, take the ring away from him, and turn it over to the Glorious Leader Sauron, who is of course more equal than his fellow Central Committee members, Saruman and the Ringwraiths. Clearly Sam's revolutionary indoctrination has been incorrect."

We then turn the hat around backwards and do the Libertarian version:

"The War of the Ring is wasteful and unnecessary. Let the *market* take care of it. Allow free competition, unhampered by government interference, and if the people want Good, they will choose Good."

There is also a Freudian version. There's this *ring,* you see, which is penetrated, and this *sword* which is broken but then restored . . . need we say any more?

Several more interpretations later, someone piped up, "But of course you cannot appreciate *The Lord of the Rings* until you have read it in the original Klingon." Much laughter follows. The Klingon version (possibly intended as an opera) also seems to be about heroic Orcs, who regain their honor by embracing death in the last, glorious battle after the destruction of Sauron, rather than surrendering to weak and honorless humans and Elves.

This is very much reminiscent of the commentary to the restored Klingon translation of *Hamlet* put out by the Klingon Language Institute . . . but we won't go into that here.

The serious question raised is this: What does a story *mean* and who knows it?

If you take seriously Deconstruction, Post-Structuralism, and other academic fads of recent decades — and we do not — then the answer would have to be that *nobody* does, except maybe the critic whose revolutionary indoctrination has been correct . . . er, we mean someone who has mastered the arcane code-language of this sort of criticism and now isn't able to speak to anybody else. (Do you know what happens when the Mafia discovers Deconstruction? They make you an offer you can't understand.)

Well, never mind that. We will grant that there is such a thing as subtextual or even unconscious meaning. Did Bram Stoker really understand the sexual dynamic of *Dracula*? Recall Tim Powers's witty remark in the interview in *Weird Tales*® 229 that the book is not so much about the oppression of Victorian women as "about a guy who lives forever by drinking blood. Don't take my word for it. Read the book. It is." At the same time, is it possible that the power of this book (which continues to fascinate when most of Stoker's other work is no more than a curiosity today), stems precisely from its ability to tap into the subconscious fears, dreams, and desires of millions of people?

For that matter, for all that Tolkien explicitly denied that *The Lord of the Rings* is allegory, it is hard to deny that the great, epic War of the Ring against the forces of darkness echoes the 20th century's two world wars. Tolkien himself was a veteran of the Battle of the Somme, perhaps the most terrible and gruel-

STAFF:
Publishers: Warren Lapine & Angela Kessler and John Gregory Betancourt
Editors: George H. Scithers & Darrell Schweitzer
Managing Editor: Carol Adams. Art Editor: Diane Weinstein; Assistant Editors: Kyle Phillips, Robert Waters, Joseph McCabe, Tim W. Burke, Myke Cole, Rocky Morrow, & Steve McDonald.
Typesetting: John Gregory Betancourt and the Owlswick & Wildside Presses

MANUSCRIPT SUBMISSIONS:
Before sending us your manuscript, please send us a business-sized envelope, with postage affixed, addressed to you, for our guidelines. The address for this and all other editorial matters:
Weird Tales®, 123 Crooked Lane, King of Prussia PA 19406–2570
Visit our message board: http://www.wildsidepress.com
An e-mail version of our guidelines is also available for the asking from WEIRDTALES@COMCAST.NET
The address for subscriptions, subscribers' changes of address, advertising, and money matters is:
DNA Publications, Inc., PO Box 2988, Radford VA 24143–2988
Visit us on the Web at: DNAPUBLICATIONS.COM

Of course we read unsolicited submissions — but only by mail in standard manuscript format. To survive, all editors insist on a few Rules: each submission must be in proper format and must include a return envelope, addressed to you, with enough U.S. Postage affixed to bring the manuscript back to you. If you want us to discard the manuscript if we don't buy it, tell us so. In that case include a business-sized envelope, addressed to you, with U.S. Postage affixed, so we can send you our comments. No loose stamps, please.

We recommend two books on writing: *On Writing Science Fiction: the Editors Strike Back!* by Scithers, Schweitzer, & John M. Ford; $19.50, postpaid, in hardcovers from Owlswick Press, 123 Crooked Lane, King of Prussia PA 19406–2750. (We wrote it, so of course we speak highly of it.) In Pennsylvania, add $1.19 sales tax. The other is the always essential *The Elements of Style*, by William Strunk, Jr., & E.B. White, available from any good bookstore.

We are not responsible for manuscripts in our hands or in transit.
You must put your *name* and *address* on the first page of every manuscript. For all manuscripts:

`use 12-point type`

`on 24-point spacing, please!`

SPICE UP YOUR READING!

WILDSIDE PULP CLASSICS: PULP FACSIMILE SERIES

Series editor: John Gregory Betancourt

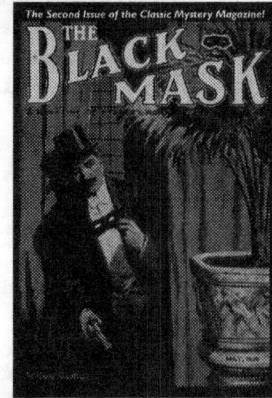

#1: Spicy Mystery Stories (August 1935)

The August 1935 issue includes contributions from Robert Leslie Bellem, Atwater Culpepper, Ellery Watson Calder, Carl Moore, E. Hoffman Price, Jerome Severs Perry, Don King, Charles R. Allen, Charles A. Baker, Jr., and Arthur Wallace.

#2: Ghost Stories (June 1931)

This issue features contributions from Conrad Richter (best known as the author of The Light in the Forest) and a story by E. and H. Heron (pen name for Mrs. Kenneth and Mr. Hesketh Prichard) featuring their psychic detective, Flaxman Low.

#3: Spicy Mystery Stories (February 1937)

The February 1937 issue features Robert Leslie Bellem, Lew Merrisll (Victor Rousseau) Hugh Speer, Justin Case (Hugh B. Cave), and many others — plus all the classic "spicy" artwork!

#4: Strange Tales #7 (January 1933)

Strange Tales combined the supernatural horror and fantasy of Weird Tales with vigorous action plots. The January 1933 issue features Hugh B. Cave's classic "Murgunstrumm," as well as stories by Robert E. Howard, Henry S. Whitehead, and many more.

#5: The Black Mask #2 (May 1920)

The rare second issue of the legendary mystery magazine!

----

ing military encounter in history. Everybody he knew in the army was killed. He only survived because he was lucky enough to be invalided out in the nick of time with trench fever. (For more about this, see *Tolkien and the Great War* by John Garth, Houghton Mifflin, 2003.)

Allegory or not, surely *The Lord of the Rings* resonated with many people because they associated with it some of the same emotional response they had from experiencing (or at least reading about) the Free World's vast struggle to remain free in the face of the gathering Shadow of the Dark Lord in the East, whether that Dark Lord might be the Kaiser, Hitler, or Stalin. Likewise, a lot of people have seen vampirism as a metaphor for forbidden sexuality, and for underground lifestyles.

These things fit, and resonate, whether the author had them in mind or not.

Sometimes an author can deliberately put a meaning into a story and it fades away with time. We have a copy of James Branch Cabell's *Figures of Earth,* in which, where the Redeemer of Poictesme, Dom Manuel, starts rallying his followers with the slogan, "Mum with Manuel," someone has written in the margin, "Cool with Coolidge." This was a contemporary joke of the time, which the modern reader is better off without. The Cabell books are more self-contained and timeless without 1920s in-jokes.

Otherwise, we tend to think that a story means what the author says it means. There may be broader emotional associations, but, unless we were to discover some letter or diary in which L. Frank Baum says, "Yes, *The Wizard of Oz* is about William Jennings Bryan and the gold standard," we are amused by that piece in *Uncle John's Bathroom Reader,* but not really convinced.

The problems of literary interpretation are complex. Whenever somebody says they have the One Answer, as the Deconstructionists seem to (inasmuch as anyone can understand them), we should become very suspicious. Certainly there are pitfalls to be avoided. It *is* possible to read entirely too much into a story, particularly if you try to discover the opinions of the author in the actions of his characters.

On this note, we must quote a letter we have received from **Ed Birchmore,** who writes:

I agree with Steve Allys who, quoting HPL, stated that some of his words are "not exactly the sentiments of an atheist." I will go further and say that Grandpa, at one time, had serious theistic sympathies and never escaped being seriously conflicted about God. In "Psychopompos" he alludes to "The Savior's image and the Cross divine" which save villagers from unholy creatures. In "Nemesis," in which he sees the "black planets roll without aim," this bleak cosmicism is modified by an admission of guilt, "Oh, great was the sin of my spirit." Sin? There is "Old Christmas" in which he refers to "the glad rites of Christ's nativity" etc. Referring to a cleric in "New England Fallen," he wrote, "Blest was that parson, noblest of mankind; true his belief, exalted was his mind." Even the redoubtable Joshi was nonplussed by these effusions and wrongly dismissed them as anomalies in his biography. We would expect Mel Gibson to be the author of such lines, not HPL. His tales are peopled with benevolent and prescient clergymen like the Rev. Abijah Hoadley, Father Iwanicki, the Rev. Dr. Checkley, and Father Merluzzo who prayed against the haunter from the stars. In the dream later published as "The Evil Clergyman" we have a classic gothic doppleganger story in which we can see the results of bad religion. HPL professed anti-religious views but it's clear that his conscience bothered him about this to the end. When the haunter comes after Blake, it's Conscience with a capital C coming after Lovecraft. Even in his later correspondence with Helly Sully it's clear that he was still wrestling with the issue of God. The conflicted theism in Lovecraft goes far beyond the issue of the gods of the Mythos. The leprous spawn of atheism have misrepresented the Old Gent from Providence in their critical writings. Not so HPL himself, though. To his eternal credit, perhaps, he remained haunted and conflicted about his deicidal tendencies. He didn't embrace the loathsome Azathoth the way many modern Lovecraftians have.

Your reading of "The Haunter of the Dark" is certainly a novel one, but we're not sure it's a valid insight.

We got a response from **S.T. Joshi** himself about this, who points out that *"It is of course very dangerous to argue from a writer's fiction what his/her philosophy is. The whole procedure is immensely fraught with pitfalls."*

Indeed it is. Do not confuse a character's opinions with those of the author. Otherwise you will come to the inevitable conclusion, on the basis of the Sherlock Holmes stories, that A. Conan Doyle was a steely-minded rationalist and not a man who believed in spirit-rappings and fairies. Likewise, all the examples cited above from Lovecraft's work can be easily explained away. A lot of the benevolent clergymen (very minor figures, most of them) are quaint figures of tradition, as ineffectual in dealing with the real universe as were the various pious foreigners who attempted to keep the Haunter of the Dark away with prayers. (You will recall how well *that* worked.)

Lovecraft's letters, written to friends and never intended for publication, are a little more reliable as a source for Lovecraft's true feelings and ideas. A passage that immediately sprang to mind was from a letter Lovecraft wrote to Maurice Moe in 1918 (*Selected Letters I,* page 60) in which HPL remarks that what he "has against religion" is that "the Judeo-Christian mythology is NOT TRUE," and then goes on for several pages in that vein, for all he says he "cannot deny" the good social effects of Christianity, though he finds them "somewhat overrated."

Joshi brings another such letter to our attention, Lovecraft writing to Robert E. Howard in 1932 (*Selected Letters IV,* p. 57):

"All I can say is that I think it is damned unlikely that anything like a cosmic central will, a spirit world, or an eternal survival of personality exists. These are the most preposterous and unjustified of all guesses which can be made about the universe, and I am not enough of a hairsplitter to pretend that I don't regard them as arrant and negligible moonshine. In theory I am an agnostic, but pending the appearance of rational evidence I must be classed, practically and provisionally, as an atheist. The chances of theism's truth being to my mind so microscopically small, I would be a pedant and a hypocrite to call myself anything else."

Not only does that show a consistency of opinion over 14 years, but Lovecraft's letters, essays, and autobiographical writings make it very, very clear that, aside from a brief childhood

fancy that he thought he saw fawns and dryads in the Rhode Island woods (at about age 7), he never entertained *any* religious beliefs at all, conventional or otherwise. He liked old churches, a charming part of old New England, but there is no convincing evidence that he ever believed in God or felt conflicted about this. Any competent Lovecraftian can quote "chapter and verse" endlessly against your thesis. The 1918 letter to Moe is largely about how morality and social order may be separated from religion itself, and how we must find a way to do this because, "The time is coming when the old formulae will cease to enchant, for nothing can last eternally which is not founded on demonstrable truth." In other words, Lovecraft believed that religion would eventually become obsolete and fade away.

As for "Psychopompos," this is a narrative poem, set in France in the Middle Ages (a period Lovecraft regarded as a time of darkness and superstition), and so *of course* the narrative viewpoint and the characters put some stock in Christian pieties, but the power of Lovecraft's horror fiction generally stems precisely from the fact that he and most of his characters do not. Lovecraft faced what Nietzsche called "the abyss," the yawning nothingness that confronts us in a vast universe *without* a deity who happens to notice that one grain of sand amid the billions happens to be inhabited.

The Most Popular Story in issue #334 was newcomer Myke Cole's "A Place for Heroes," with Charles L. Harness's "In the Catacombs" second and Darrell Schweitzer's "Lord Abernaeven's Tale" a close third. "Cthulwhat?" by Joshua Rupp also drew a lot of praise. The reprint feature, with W.C. Morrow's "Over The Absinthe Bottle" was generally well-received, and inspired this letter from **Earl P. Dean:**

Recently I read the W.C. Morrow story that you reprinted in your magazine. I am among many readers who noticed how similar the events in "Over the Absinthe Bottle" were to Ambrose Bierce's "An Occurrence at Owl Creek Bridge." In both tales, the main character is in a dangerous situation and plotting desperately to find a way out. In the Morrow, the main character joins a person for a drink, whom he takes to be a sort of philanthropist. He is starving and enters an all-or-nothing bet to gain control of a large sum of money, therefore alleviating the starvation. In the Bierce tale, the main character is trying to figure out how he can extricate himself from a hanging. The parallels continue in both tales. The resemblances are so

striking that I couldn't help wondering if there was a history between these two men regarding the tales.

Certainly we can see the resemblance, particularly in the subjective, then in the cruelly objective endings of both stories. Yes, Bierce and Morrow knew one another, were friends, and were part of the same San Francisco literary scene in the late 19th century. Most of the information available about Morrow can be found in Sam Moskowitz's essay on him in Darrell Schweitzer's *Discovering Classic Horror Fiction* (now in print from Wildside Press). It had formerly been believed that Morrow was a follower of Bierce, but Moskowitz established that Morrow was writing this kind of story first, and in fact was an editor who bought many early Bierce stories for San Francisco publications. According to S.T. Joshi and David Schultz's bibliography of Bierce, "An Occurrence at Owl Creek Bridge" first appeared in 1890. The Morrow story first appeared in *The Argonaut* in 1893. In this case it would seem that Bierce influenced Morrow.

Thomas Fuchs writes: *John Gregory Betancourt thinks "copyright should be rolled back to life-plus-20 years." I ask him and your readers to consider two scenarios. In one, a musket-toting European blasts a couple of Indians, claims their land for his king and himself, and passes the title of this land through dozens of generations. Alternatively, a writer or other artist sits himself down, creates something out of his own imagination, harms no one, and Mr. Betancourt wants to deprive his heirs of the benefits of this effort a mere 20 years after the artist's death. Is this fair?*

The point Betancourt was getting at in his column in issue

334 was that, if there is no active estate and thus no one to license rights from, copyright laws might cause an author's works to perish by keeping them out of print for so long that they do not have a chance to influence the culture: by the time they are in the public domain they're too obsolete to matter. Imagine a scenario in which the works of Edgar Allan Poe were kept out of print for seventy years after his death — until 1919. Imagine the effect on weird fiction and literature in general if Poe had not been available except to antiquarians for all that time. Maybe the copyright law needs to be changed to hold publishers blameless when they reprint work belonging to apparently abandoned literary estates. Of course, they should be obligated to pay royalties, but not damages, if such an estate eventually surfaces.

Jason Hardy writes: *The fine cover by Plumridge captured the tone of Weird Tales perfectly. And having a woman artist contribute the cover hearkened back to the Brundage days. Many of the stories in WT have a nice dark "theatrical" tone and I thought the cover fit well with that. The interior "stable" of artists (Barr, Fabian, etc.) are some of the best in the fantasy business. Especially Fabian who is an experienced pro and frequently contributes an illustration as strong or stronger than the tale he is illustrating. I particularly liked the title bar he produced for the contents page. The mermaid is a nice touch.*

By far the strongest story in the issue was Darrell Schweitzer's "Lord Abernaeven's Tale." Very well written and creative (especially the tapestry idea). He is very good at blending fantasy and horror in his stories. As with

many of the best WT writers he has created believable, very detailed fantasy worlds and revisited them.

From Robert Howard forward this has been one of the best things about WT. I truly miss, for example, the great Fritz Leiber and his frequent visits to Lankhmar. What your magazine provides are similar examples and they are appreciated.

Richard Gallagher writes: Your editorial observations about the decline of horror struck home. As a subscriber to both Night Cry and Twilight Zone magazines way back when, I recall how the latter issues tended to be a bit pretentious (especially TZ) instead of going for the gut reaction a good horror story will aim for. This may sound like I'm stereotyping the genre, so please note that I do believe a horror story can be crafted as well as any literary fiction out there. Conversely, I attribute the decline of horror to an overdose of schlock and sequels with cardboard characters, hackneyed plots, overemphasis on blood and gore instead of the characters' reactions to whatever the "horror" was, and countless others I'm sure you're aware of.

Indeed, this can happen in any field, as the publishers try to isolate the "active ingredient" that makes a type of book successful, and wind up with something so narrowly defined that it becomes mere repetition. This works . . . for a very short time. It can generate a bestseller or two, but then the sales begin to rapidly fall off. Even as the success of Stephen King may have created the boom in the horror field in the late '80s, too many attempts to replicate that success caused the bust ten years later, from which we have not yet recovered.   Ω

THE ADVENTURES OF DOCTOR ESZTERHAZY
by **Avram Davidson**, with full-color dust jacket by **George Barr**,
interior drawings by **Todd Cameron Hamilton**, & a foreword by **Gene Wolfe**.

Tom Whitmore, in *Locus, the Newspaper of the Science Fiction Field,* wrote: "But what about these stories, I hear you ask. What are they about, and why should I read them? They are about Engelbert Eszterhazy, possessor of six doctorates; they are about the empire of Scythia-Pannonia-Transbalkania and its tribulations; they are about wonder, marvel, and the unexpected.

"They are Victorian tales, with a Victorian pace, with the richness of language that makes the best Victoriana so marvelous, and with modern allusions and understanding lurking just beneath the surface; to try to summarize them individually is

to wreak havoc on their integrity. There are wonders here for those who know a little, and marvels for those who know a lot, about literature, history, botany, or any other subject.

"But you should read these stories because they are fun. They amuse, instruct, alert, puzzle, and challenge in the way that only great stories can. The publisher's conceit of having each story identified by an icon rather than a running title is totally appropriate. . . . A masterful performance from both author and publisher!"

Analog Science Fiction & Fact wrote: "Between 1974 and 1986, Avram Davidson published a number of stories of such astonishing skill, erudition, wit, and quirkiness that major markets such as *The New Yorker* and *Playboy* wouldn't touch them with a ten-foot Bulgarian. Set on the cusp between the nineteenth and the twentieth centuries in Scythia-Pannonia-Transbalkania, the fourth largest empire in Europe (the Turks were fifth) and a literal neighbor of the comic-opera realms of Graustark and Ruritania, flavored with Gilbert & Sullivan, Twain, Chesterton, and Conan Doyle (*et* only Davidson knows the *cetera*), they starred Engelbert Eszterhazy as a gentleman in search of learning wherever he might find it, unfazed by the strangest of events, cleverly combining the data that came his way to solve mysteries and ease the lots of the polyglot peoples of the empire. . . . Buy it."

Hardcover, 386 pages: $24.50 postpaid, from Owlswick Press, 123 Crooked Lane, King of Prussia PA 19406-2570.

Name:_____

Address:_____

More address:_____

City/State/ZIP:_____

THE DEN

by John Gregory Betancourt

It seems we are in a veritable new golden age of small press publishing. Not only are the classic older small presses (such as Arkham House, Donald M. Grant, W. Paul Ganley, etc.) still producing excellent books, but a new crop of small presses has sprung up to continue the tradition. In this column, we will take a look at one of my favorites: Hippocampus Press.

Hippocampus founder Derrick Hussey has created a distinctive line of books mostly related to classic horror in the Lovecraftian mode — with occasional forays into weird fantasy. Longtime fans will, of course, realize that this is ground originally covered by Arkham House. But Arkham, under the 1990s editorship of James Turner, abandoned that niche and focused more on contemporary science fiction and fantasy (publishing authors such as Lucius Shepard, Greg Bear, Ian R. MacLeod, etc.) There was clearly a need for a company like Hippocampus to pitch in and keep Lovecraft publishing alive. But in recent years, Peter Ruber, the latest Arkham editor, has turned the company back in its original direction most satisfactorily, releasing such worthwhile books as *The Selected Letters of Clark Ashton Smith* and a new printing of the great retrospective collection of Smith's fiction, *A Rendezvous in Averoigne*.

Is there still a need for Hippocampus? I think so. Hussey is not just publishing books by writers of interest to fans of classic horror, but he is providing an important venue for scholarly and critical works as well.

Take a look at a partial list of Hippocampus's past releases:

• 5 volumes of Lovecraft's *Collected Essays* (the first 3 are already out), edited by S.T. Joshi
• *The Shadow out of Time: The Corrected Text,* by H.P. Lovecraft
• *From the Pest Zone: The New York Stories,* by H.P. Lovecraft
• *The Annotated Fungi from Yuggoth,* by H.P. Lovecraft
• *The Annotated Supernatural Horror in Literature,* by H.P. Lovecraft
• *Lovecraft's Library: A Catalogue,* edited by S.T. Joshi
• *The Black Diamonds* by Clark Ashton Smith
• *The Last Oblivion: Best Fantastic Poems of Clark Ashton Smith*
• *The Sword of Zagan and Other Writings* by Clark Ashton Smith

Hippocampus's schedule of 2004 and 2005 includes:
• *An H.P. Lovecraft Encyclopedia* (April 2004)
• *Incredible Adventures* by Algernon Blackwood (June 2004)
• *Out of the Immortal Night: Selected Works of Samuel Loveman* (October 2004)
• *The House of Sounds and Others* by M. P. Shiel (January 2005)
• *H.P. Lovecraft: Letters to Rheinhart Kleiner* (March 2005)
• *Letters of George Sterling and Clark Ashton Smith* (July 2005)

CLASSIC PULP FICTION FROM WILDSIDE PRESS!

Satan's Daughter and Other Tales from the Pulps
by E. Hoffmann Price. Intro by Darrell Schweitzer

A baker's dozen of classic pulp stories, by a master of the genre! *Satan's Daughter and Other Tales from the Pulps* includes such rare gems as the title story, "Scourge of the Silver Dragon," "Revolt of the Damned," "Pit of Madness," "The Walking Dead," "Drink or Draw," and many more. A delightful selection, ranging from fantasy to horror to action-mystery, all sprinkled with a dash of erotica.

Out of the Wreck and Other Nautical Tales
by Captain A. E. Dingle

Captain A.E. Dingle published sea stories in the pulp magazines for decades, and the volume, quality and variety of his tales is nothing short of astonishing. This collection assembles eight of his finest, from the Sherlock Holmes pastiche "Watson!" to the short novel "The Coolie Ship," from the misadventures of "Skimps, Ship's Boy" to the lives of "Hard-Shell Clammers" -- nautical stories told by a master craftsman!

The Mysterious Wu Fang: Case of the Suicide Tomb
by Robert J. Hogan

The ancient tomb had been sealed for a thousand years; its discovery was an archaeological find. But few guessed its horrible secret, or knew that an Oriental super-villain, the fiendish Wu Fang, wished to enter its portals to capture the death germs buried there -- deadly germs of a rare plague of madness which he meant to use to control the world! From the December, 1935 issue of *The Mysterious Wu Fang* magazine, presented with its original cover and interior art.

Operator #5: Blood Reign of the Dictator
by Curtis Steele

Operator #5 appeared in more than 48 novels in the pulp magazine bearing his name. From April 1934 to November 1939, Jimmy Christopher fought villains from inside the United States and invaders from without. With World War II looming on the horizon, the Operator #5 books became a reflection of the times -- none more so than when a fascist dictator appears to take over the U.S. government! *Blood Reign of the Dictator* is a classic entry in the series.

Secret Agent "X": The Legions of the Living Dead
by Brant House

From the September, 1935 issue of *Secret Agent X* comes this sensational novel: "From nowhere hurtled that black death car. And from nowhere came its grisly occupants. They were not of the earth, for their human flesh was immune to bullets. They were not of the grave, for they manned the wheel and a blasting machine gun- Secret Agent "X" made a desperate maneuver to block their invasion of the land of the living. And in that weird terror trap, he came face to face with a man he knew had died five years ago!"

If anything, Hippocampus isn't so much competing with Arkham House as supplementing it, much the way Necronomicon Press did years ago. (Necronomicon Press, if not dead, is at least severely moribund these days. Hippocampus has even picked up the magazine *Lovecraft Studies*, formerly published by Necronomicon, and released a new double issue, #42-43.)

A few of my favorite Hippocampus releases:

The Pleasures of a Futuroscope, by Lord Dunsany
Hippocampus, 200 pages, $32.95 (hardcover)
Written circa 1955, this science fiction novel — one of the last of Dunsany's major works — remained unpublished until 2003, when it was discovered among his papers. This is one of those horrors-of-the-atomic-age stories, where the narrator, using a futuroscope, peers into the future and witnesses humanity after an atomic war. With London reduced to a crater, everything seems hopeless. But he begins to follow the struggle of a single family to survive.

As SF, it's decided minor stuff; but one reads Dunsany not for the scientific content but for the grace and poetry of his language. As *The Pleasures of a Futuroscope* shows, his descriptive powers remained powerful to the end of his career.

Recommended mostly for readers who have already gone through all the classic Dunsany fantasies and want more.

The Thirst of Satan, by George Sterling
Hippocampus, 216 pages, $15.00
Dedicated fans of Clark Ashton Smith will probably recognize Sterling's name, for he was Smith's poetic mentor; and indeed Smith's correspondence with Sterling forms an important part of Arkham House's *The Selected Letters of Clark Ashton Smith*. Unfortunately, Sterling is largely unknown today; poetry as a field has become a niche interest, and the California Romantics (from early 20th Century poets like Smith and Sterling to their current descendants, Donald Sidney-Fryer and others) have long been unjustly neglected.

Much of Sterling's work here is clearly of interest to fans of weird fantasy. Take, for instance, "The Summer of the Gods"—

Methought in dream I saw Ulysses bold —
Lured by strange music to the hidden West —
Pass onward in that memorable quest
Of islands where the demigods of old
Beyond the portals of Elysium hold
The twilight and the threnodies of rest.
Great gleamed the sunset upon ocean's breast
And all those urgent oars cast up its gold.

Hushed are the voices of the mythic dales
And lost the days whose dawn and eve of yore
Held a mystery whose kindly veils
Fell as a radiance on sea and shore,
Whose eastward moons and suns departing bore
A glory unto fat, intrepid sails.

Romantic, indeed, conjuring wonderful visions for anyone familiar with the Odyssey. Highly recommended for those sick of modern non-metrical poetry.

The Shadow Out of Time: *The Corrected Text,* by H.P. Lovecraft
Hippocampus, 136 pages, $15.00 (trade paper)

As all Lovecraft fans probably know, "The Shadow Out of Time" was Lovecraft's last major work, published in *Astounding Stories* in June 1936

the only authoritative version of this classic story. Paragraphing has been restored to Lovecraft's original, two dozen words have been changed, and six lines of omitted text have been restored. Minor things, yes, but important since the movement in Lovecraft scholarship has been to put things back exactly as Lovecraft intended them.

The Sword of Zagan and Other Writings, by Clark Ashton Smith
   Hippocampus Press, 182 pages, $15.00

At 39,000 words, *The Sword of Zagan* qualifies (barely) as a novel. It was found among Smith's papers at the John Hay Library at Brown University (along with the 100,000-word novel *The Black Diamonds* and various other unpublished works — mostly juvenilia). Still, any new works by Smith are of interest, even minor ones written as a teenager, as these are. The book's theme is generally Eastern, with *The Sword of Zagan* being an Arabian Nights-style tale following two janissaries in their adventures, and nearly a dozen short stories (some fragmentary) set in India and the Middle East. The introduction by S.T. Joshi and notes by editor Dr. W.C. Farmer are fascinating.

If you've read Smith's Arkham House volume, *A Rendezvous in Averoigne*, and the few other in-print books of Smith's work, *The Sword of Zagan* is a fun follow-up.   Ω

with all the usual editorial meddling. With the recent discovery of an original handwritten copy of the manuscript, editors S.T. Joshi and David E. Schultz have prepared what must be considered

THE GHOST OF ME

by Melinda Thielbar

illustrated by Allen Koszowski

The ghost of O'Hare airport appears as a pretty young woman, probably in her twenties, wearing business attire. She's a friendly ghost, and a helpful one. Many travelers claim she's given them directions that helped them make tight connections. One man says she caught him before he tripped down an escalator, saving him and the people below him from a nasty fall. She's usually seen in Terminal One, but she has been spotted in other places. In one notable tale, she stopped a mugger who was running through Parking Lot A. No one knows what she said to him, but whatever it was, it made him drop the purse he was carrying and turn himself in. She looks as real as any other business traveler while doing her good deed, but when the beneficiary tries to thank her, she always smiles and then vanishes.

There are at least a dozen origin stories for every one ghost, and the ghost of O'Hare is no exception. "She's our daughter who died in a plane crash." "She's my sister who went to school in Chicago." "She's my girlfriend who was supposed to meet me in Chicago but died on the way." None of these stories are true. I know because I know who she is. She's a ghost of me.

I have always been precocious. In school, I skipped a grade not once, but twice. I flew through college in three years, and then for good measure, I got a master's degree in one. By age twenty-two, I was working for one of the largest consulting firms in the country, and by age twenty-four, I was managing one of our most important projects, building a database for one of our biggest clients. I often traveled to their headquarters in Cincinnati and worked long hours to satisfy my increasing responsibilities and shortening deadlines. By age twenty-five, I was in the hospital with a hole in my stomach. I spent two weeks lying on my back, listening to doctors lecture on bland diets, regular exercise, and avoiding stress.

While in the hospital, I did a careful benefit-cost analysis of my current job, and I realized that I could afford to take a job with substantially less salary as long as it had regular hours and no travel. As a shining example of the efficiency that had made me a valuable employee, I wrote a letter of resignation my first day back at work. My boss was not impressed. He tried to bribe me to stay, offering more money and a bigger office. I turned him down. He tried to appeal to my conscience, saying we were in the middle of a big project and it was unfair of me to leave. I pointed out that we were always in the middle of a big project. Three weeks after I tendered my resignation, he was down to threats and making dire predictions about my chances of finding another job. I thanked him for his concern, informed him that I had accepted an offer from one of his former clients, and promised to keep in touch as I dropped my nameplate in the trash.

Maintaining a database is much easier than building one, and I settled into the new job quickly. Once I had my feet under me, I started making other changes. The new office was close to the L, so I sold the hunter green convertible I never had time to drive. Because I was going home on time, I didn't have to be as close to work, so I moved to a part of the city with cheaper rent and friendlier neighbors. I could no longer afford the health club I never had time to attend, but the daily walk to and from the train helped me lose ten pounds.

Everything would have been perfect if I hadn't been both unlucky and dumb. I was unlucky because someone lifted my purse out of my backpack about a week before I moved. I was dumb because I didn't realize the purse was gone until the next day. When I couldn't find it in my apartment or at any of the places I had been the night before, I called my credit card companies. No one besides me had used the cards, so I ordered new ones and forgot about it in the chaos of selling half of my life and moving the rest to the North side of Chicago.

The new apartment had its expected collection of difficulties. I spent a day at home waiting for the phone repairman, an evening hammering at windows that had been painted shut, and a Saturday afternoon clearing the storage of items the former tenants had deemed important enough to keep but not important enough to move. It was three days before I noticed I wasn't getting any mail. I wasn't worried; the Chicago mail system moves at the approximate speed of glacial ice, but when I had been living at the new address for a week without so much as a pre-approved MasterCard offer, I called the post office.

"Hello, I'm calling to make sure my mail was forwarded properly," I said.

Keyboard sounds followed by a woman's voice asking for my name and address.

I gave them and waited. After a few minutes, she said, "Was that the old address, you gave me, ma'am?"

"No," I said. "My old address was 236 West Diversey Parkway. My new address is 5200 North Ravenswood."

Another pause. "Now, this is weird," she said. "We're forwarding mail from the Ravenswood address to the Diversey address."

I made the logical assumption that this was a post office screw-up. "Can you change it to be forwarded to 5200 North Ravenswood instead?"

She could, and she did, promising that my mail would soon arrive in the proper location.

I thanked her, hung up, and dialed the management office of my old building to see if they had my mail. After a few minutes of being transferred from office to office (it was a big building), I had the mailroom.

"We haven't seen any mail for you here," the clerk told me after I'd explained the problem.

"Maybe you put it in the new tenant's box by mistake?" I asked helpfully.

She gave a small snort to tell me I'd insulted her. "That apartment's vacant and there's no mail in the box."

"The apartment's vacant?" I asked. For the area I had been living in, the rent on my old apartment was cheap.

Sound of papers shuffling. "There was some vandalism after you moved out. They're making repairs."

"Oh. Well, if you do get some mail for me, please call me at this number."

"Of course, Ma'am. Have a nice day."

* * *

A few days later, my mail arrived as promised. It wasn't worth the wait: junk mail and the bill for a Bloomingdales card. Now, I'd shredded the Bloomies card when I stopped wearing suits to work, but a bill with my name and a forwarding mark on it appeared just the same. I scratched my head for a few minutes, then remembered that my

Social Security card had been in the lost purse. After I stopped swearing, I called Bloomingdales customer service, where I was informed that I had opened a new account soon after closing my old one. I informed them that I hadn't and that my purse had been stolen recently. (OK, so I'd probably lost it, but there was no need to tell *them* that.) They canceled the card, but they wouldn't cancel the charges until they could match my signature with the signature on the credit application. If the signatures didn't match, they would believe I hadn't opened the account. I swore again (silently) and gave them my address so they could send me a notary form.

A Victoria's Secret bill arrived the next day, followed by bills from Marshall Fields and Nordstroms. Lord & Taylor, Macy's, and the Waterford store came the next week. Each card had only a few charges, as if the person who'd applied for it had only used it for a day's shopping, and each card was from a store where I'd shopped in the days when I could afford them. When I got the Best Buy bill, I started getting curious.

"Can you tell me what they bought with it?" I asked the customer service representative.

There was a few seconds of keyboard noise as he punched it up. "Hand Pilot Vy with a hard case and a service contract," he said.

I felt a chill as I looked down at the Hand Vy with a hard case that I'd bought in my future-corporate-executive days. "Is that still the latest model?"

"Lady, this is credit services, not the catalog."

"Right," I said. "Sorry. Do you have the address they gave for the service contract?"

He read off my old address. "You want me to cancel this card?"

"Yeah," I sighed. "And send a notary form so I can prove it wasn't me."

"I looked it up on their online catalog," I told Barb at dinner that night. "It was the latest model, except for the one that has a built-in cell phone."

Barb was the only friend I had kept from my former life. We'd met at a software conference and bonded immediately when we realized we'd both learned to program in the same obscure language. We lived a few blocks apart. We frequented the same clubs. We liked the same movies. I watched Barb's cats when she was on vacation. She picked up my mail when I traveled for work. After I moved, we set up a standing date for dinner every

Friday at an Italian place downtown, close to both of our offices. I'd been giving her weekly updates on the stolen wallet situation.

Now, she was looking at me skeptically over a piece of pasta. "And?" she asked.

"Nothing except that I have the same model."

Barb rolled her eyes. "So you have the same taste in electronics as the person who stole your purse."

"But don't you think it's weird they're only taking out credit cards from stores where *I* used to have credit cards?" I asked.

"Are you saying you have a credit card stalker?"

"Well, no," I muttered and picked at the food on my plate. "But it could be identity theft or something. Couldn't it?"

"Identity theft is when they use your information to take out credit cards, which they have done, and open bank accounts, which they have not. Shopping at your favorite stores doesn't count."

"Former favorite stores," I corrected. "I don't shop at those places anymore."

"Whatever." Barb tore a piece of bread and ran it through the sauce on her plate. "Look, Karen, it's not like you shopped at really weird places. It's a coincidence. Forget about it and finish your ravioli."

I did. Smart people take good advice.

It took weeks to collect all my forms and mail them back out. By the time I put the last one in the mail, I got a reply from Bloomingdales. The news was not good.

"What do you mean the signatures match?" I asked the Bloomingdales credit services representative. "That's impossible."

"All I can tell you, Miss Anderson, is according to our handwriting expert, your signature and the signature on the credit card application are the same." The Bloomingdales credit fraud investigator had been much more sympathetic the first time we'd spoken.

"Isn't it possible that the person responsible faked my signature?" I asked, doing my best to maintain righteous indignation.

"It's possible, Miss Anderson, but it isn't very likely."

I summoned my diplomatic voice. "I didn't open that account. How do I prove it?"

The rest of the conversation did not go well. I could send them a police report proving that my purse had been stolen, except I hadn't filed a police report because I had assumed my purse was lost. I could also provide an alibi for the day the card application was filed, but since I wasn't traveling on business anymore, it would be hard to prove I hadn't been at Bloomingdales. After ten minutes of fruitless conversation, I gave up trying to convince the investigator I wasn't a deadbeat, wrote down the date the application was filed, and hung up.

The other handwriting experts agreed with Bloomingdales. Not only had my purse been stolen, it had been stolen by someone who liked all my favorite stores and knew how to fake my signature. Then the bill for a Consolidated Airlines Visa card arrived.

Consolidated had been my airline of choice when I was traveling. I'd been planning to get a credit card from them but had never gotten around to it. I can't say I was surprised as I scanned down the list of places where it had been used. There were charges from the grocery store in my old apartment building, the restaurant next to the old office, and the drugstore that had been between work and home. There was a week's worth of charges in Cincinnati, where I used to go on business, and one large charge to my mechanic. I glanced at the calendar. If I'd still had the car, it would have been time for a tune-up.

I left the bill on my desk and started cleaning the apartment. I always clean when I'm thinking because it's something useful I can do that leaves my brain free. I washed dishes (the new place didn't have a dishwasher) and thought about the last few months, the free evenings, the relaxing weekends. I thought about riding the train to and from work and the car I had sold. I realized I didn't miss anything about my former job.

But I'd enjoyed my first job until I got sick. The work had been challenging. Challenge was something severely lacking in my new job, and I had always been easily bored. It seemed odd, now that I thought about it.

The next day, I called my new boss to tell her I was sick. Then, I called my old boss. He sounded genuinely pleased to hear from me. I learned that he was in the middle of a project which he felt was desperately understaffed; it took him all of ten seconds to try another recruiting pitch.

"You're sure you don't miss us, Karen? Your old office is still open."

I laughed. "Why is that, Dan? No one wants an office by the window?"

He laughed, too. "Actually, it's had a few problems since you left."

"Problems?" I echoed, trying to sound only a little curious.

"Yeah, darndest thing. Somebody vandalized it a few days after you left. They broke the chair, turned the desk over, and scribbled on the walls with your permanent markers. We had to repaint and order new furniture. Then, Tammy moved in, but she couldn't get the network connection to work. The computer kept logging in and out randomly. Ted thinks he has it fixed, but Tammy hasn't moved back in yet."

"That's weird," I said. "Any of the other offices have that problem?"

"Nope. Guess the place misses you," Dan said brightly. "You should come back."

"Not a chance."

I stared at the phone for a long time after I hung up.

Do I believe in ghosts? I know I do now. Did I believe in them that morning? Probably not. I read my share of ghost stories when I was a kid, and I had about a dozen *Twilight Zone* tapes I'd bought in college, but I'd never *believed* any of it. I told myself I was going in to work as I got dressed and rode the L downtown, but I knew I was lying. I got off at Clark and Lake, two stops before my regular one, and switched to the Blue Line, the train that would take me to the airport. It was like peeking for the monster under the bed. It's impossible for a monster to be there, but you look anyway because you need to *know* it's not. That's how I felt as I rode the L along the expressway. I was leaning over the edge of the bed so I could peek underneath and reassure myself there was nothing there.

I hadn't been to the airport since I'd left my old job. My backpack suddenly felt too light without my laptop computer, and I felt naked as I stood in line at the ticket counter without luggage. I presented my credit card and ID at the desk and asked for a fully-refundable ticket for an evening flight. The ticket agent looked at me suspiciously when I told her I didn't have anything to check. I showed her my backpack. "I'm going home to my parents." I looked young enough to get away with that. "My clothes are there." She shrugged, muttered something about rich brats, and booked the flight.

Airport security may be tighter than it used

to be, but once you're past the metal detectors, it's the same as always. They frisked me and hand-checked my backpack because the same-day ticket purchase had raised a red flag, but no one bothered me as I zigzagged through the terminals. I made sure I walked past all the places that had been my favorites. I checked the ATM at the B gates, the Starbucks just before the tunnel to C, and the McDonald's just after the tunnel. Nothing. I rode the moving walkway under the Pink Floyd light show twice. I walked to the gate where the morning Cincinnati flight was due to take off. I checked the McDonald's and the Starbucks near the gates. Nothing. I was thinking of excuses I could use to get into my old office alone when a billboard for the Consolidated Visa card reminded me of my new Consolidated Visa.

I had always meant to get a Consolidated credit card but hadn't. Another thing I had always meant to do was buy a membership in the Consolidated Travelers Club. They had a nice lounge in O'Hare with laptop hookups and electrical outlets. They even brought you soda. I checked the map and walked back to concourse A.

The lady at the Travelers Club desk was well-dressed, and she looked at me with a professional smile that took in my jeans and T-shirt without blinking. "Hello, ma'am, may I see your membership card, please?"

"I don't have it with me," I said, flashing my driver's license. "But I have a membership. My name is Karen Anderson. Frequent flyer number 330422718842."

I watched her punch the number into the computer. She frowned at her read-out, and I wondered if they registered people who visited. Was another Karen Anderson already in there? The frown disappeared and the professional smile was back when she looked at my license again. "Of course, Ms. Anderson. Please come in."

I walked past her, feeling like I had scored a minor victory. I was so pleased with myself, I almost missed what I had been looking for.

She was sitting in a quiet corner of the lounge, bent over her laptop with an intensity I remembered from not-that-long ago. She was immaculate in a pinstripe suit and blue blouse that I never would have thought to put together. Her manicured fingers were painted a subtle mauve that matched her lipstick. Her ankles were crossed under the chair, showing the toes of an expensive brand of one-inch heels.

It was my face, my hair, my body, but she was

thinner than I was even now. Her hair was about two shades lighter than mine, the color I would have dyed it if I'd been able to go to the salon every four weeks. It was styled too, turned under at just the right angle to frame her face. I always wore my hair in a ponytail when I was traveling, and I didn't wear a suit if I could help it. Even if I had to go straight from the airport to the office, I always wore my tennis shoes and changed once I got there. Even with the executive treatment, you do lot of walking at the airport.

This was me as I would have been if all the things that are supposed to matter to young professionals had mattered to me. I could see now why I was always so frustrated at my old job, and why I was always so tired. I couldn't play the game the way it was supposed to be played, so I had to work doubly hard to keep up. It must have surprised clients to find out that the girl with chipped nail polish and plain hair really did know what she was talking about.

I watched the other Karen's dancing fingers, captivated by how perfect she looked. The rhythm of her typing, and the way her eyes flicked from keyboard to screen told me she was writing a program. I walked to the table she had all to herself and sat down.

She ignored me.

I said, "Excuse me, Miss, do you have the time?"

"Eleven forty-five," she answered, glancing at the time display on her computer screen.

I waited. Finally, either curious or irritated, she looked up. "Can I help you?" My get-on-with-it voice. It was strange to be on the receiving end.

"Karen Anderson?"

"Yes," she said.

"Don't you recognize me, Karen?"

She looked me over ponytail to sneakers, and I could tell she was about to say: *No, I do not know you, you insane person, and how do you know my name?* I pulled out my driver's license.

She looked at the picture, the same picture that was on her driver's license, and froze.

"Read the name, Karen," I said quietly.

She looked at me, sudden recognition and a lot more I couldn't read in her eyes. There was fear, maybe a little guilt. Was relief there too? I thought I saw it in the moment before she pushed me.

The other Karen was quicker than I was (she'd probably been taking those cardio kick boxing classes I'd always meant to sign up for). My chair went over backwards. My feet were over my head, and I felt something in my back go *crack* as it decided it did not like moving that way. It took me a few minutes to get untangled, and when I stood up, everyone in the lounge was looking at me.

"Where did she go?" I asked. They all stared at me blankly. I turned to the man sitting closest to me.

"Let me guess. I was sitting here, talking to myself, showing my driver's license to no one, and then I pushed my own chair over backwards?"

He nodded.

"Of course I did. Thank you." I grabbed my bag and ran out the door.

She was across the hall, clutching her backpack, which looked an awful lot like mine, and watching the door to the Travelers Club. She was waiting to see if I'd follow her. She needed to look under the bed, too.

"Karen!" I called.

She bolted, running back toward the B and C concourses. I tried to chase her, but she had a big advantage. I had to dodge the people who didn't get out of my way. She just ran through them.

I wandered the airport for the rest of the day. I stood at the gate each time a Cincinnati flight left and each time a Cincinnati flight arrived. When evening came, I turned my ticket in for a refund (not to the ticket agent I'd bought it from) and moved my search to baggage claim. I stood by the carousels. I walked up and down the cab lines. She wasn't there. At nine o'clock, I got back on the L.

When the train started moving, I took my cell phone out of my backpack and called Barb.

"Hello?" Barb's voice answered on the second ring.

"Barb, it's Karen. I need a favor. Do you still have the keys to my old apartment?"

"Right here on my key chain, which reminds me that you still haven't given me copies of your new ones."

"I know. I know. Listen, I need those old keys. Can I stop by?"

"Karen, you sound weird. What's up?"

I switched the phone to the other ear, trying to make up a plausible reason that wasn't a lie. "I feel weird," I said finally. "But I think I'll be better soon."

I arrived at my old apartment building at eleven o'clock. My fingers trembled as I slid Barb's copy of my front door key into the lock, prepared to bolt if the locks had changed and I set off the alarm. The front door swung open with that slight creak the building manager had never bothered to fix. I smiled grimly, thinking of how the rental agents had praised the building's security system as I walked down the hall to the elevator. No security guard appeared to challenge me. I stepped into the elevator and punched the button for the tenth floor, still shaking. I didn't *know* she was here. She could be haunting a hotel room in Cincinnati. She could be at the office solving phantom problems on her ghostly laptop. She could be cruising Chicago in a spectral hunter green convertible, but I didn't think so. Dan had said the problems with my old office were fixed. The hotel in Cincinnati had never felt like home. The old apartment, still vacant, was the only place she could be. At least I hoped it was still vacant, or I was going to look really foolish.

The elevator doors opened with a soft chime. I looked to either side before stepping out, even though there wasn't a need. My neighbors were all professional people. They worked long hours, and were either asleep or lounging in front of the television by ten o'clock. I walked down the empty hallway to my old apartment. The nail where I'd hung my welcome wreath was still there, and the door frame was the same light purple it had been when I moved out. Everyone in the building hated that color, which was why I had kept it. I'd never liked the people in my building. I pressed my ear to the door and listened. There was no sound of the television, no radio, no hum of appliances running. I slipped my key into the lock. It turned easily, and the door opened.

The front door led straight to the living room, which had two windows looking over the street. The bedrooms were to the left, and the kitchen, which was separated from the living room by a low wall, was on the right. The light filtering in from outside was enough for me to see that the apartment was empty, or almost empty. The woman in the mailroom had said the apartment was vandalized. Dan told me someone had scribbled on my office walls with permanent marker. There were no permanent markers here, so she'd had to improvise. I could see plastic billowing over one window where she'd broken it, and as my eyes adjusted, I could make out what she had written on the walls.

Mine. Mine. Mine. This apartment is mine. The chant was inscribed over and over from the ceiling to the floor. She'd written it in all caps and in script. She'd gouged it into the plaster and printed it neatly by chipping paint one flake at a time. I stepped into the room, wishing I'd thought to bring a flashlight. The writing was the most ragged on the wall by the kitchen. She'd started there, and then, as she progressed around the living room, it got neater.

I moved to the wall facing the street where the sentences had been printed straight across the wall over and over, as neatly as if a computer had printed them. I found what I was looking for under the non-broken window. *Property of Karen J. Anderson* in cursive handwriting. My handwriting.

"I didn't think you wanted to be here." My voice.

I turned around, still crouched. She was standing by the door that led to the bedrooms, dressed for bed in satin pajamas and slippers. She had a baseball bat in one hand.

"I came to find you," I said.

"I thought you didn't want me either," she said, raising her chin defiantly. "Why else would you try to get rid of me?"

"I wasn't trying to get rid of you," I said, standing up.

"Then why am I here while you're over there?"

I didn't know how to answer that, so I tried to change the subject. "I like what you've done with the place." I gestured to the walls. "It's homey."

She glared at me. She could tell I was being sarcastic but didn't know why.

"What do you see here?" I asked her.

"What do you mean 'What do I see?' I see my apartment." She pointed to one corner. "I see the sofa I bought right after I got this job." She pointed to another corner. "I see the chair from my college dorm room. I dragged it all the way to Chicago because I didn't want to part with it. I see my books and my CD player and my television. What do *you* see?"

I looked at the marks my furniture had left on the rug. I sold the chair when I moved, but when she pointed to where it had sat for over a year, I thought I could see it again. Without looking, I reached out to my left, just where the arm of the sofa would have been, and I could feel the upholstery under my fingers. I squinted and turned my head so I was looking at the room out of the corner of my eye, and my old apartment shimmered back into view, just as it had been before I started packing.

But that was crazy. "I see an empty apartment," I said, "with *mine mine mine* scribbled on the walls."

She looked around her, blinking, and I could tell she saw what I saw for a moment, just as I had seen the chair she was pointing to. I came closer.

"When was the last time you went to the office?"

She looked at me. "I went today."

"Then why did I see you at the airport?" I asked.

She bit her lip and looked down. "I must have been coming back from Cincinnati."

"But it was in the morning, Karen," I said. "You never come back until evening."

"Then I must have been leaving."

"Then why are you here now?" I was close enough to touch her.

"I don't *know*," she said finally. "I don't *remember.*"

"I think you do. You remember getting sick, don't you?"

She nodded.

"Do you remember being in the hospital? Do you remember what the doctors told you about stress?"

She nodded again.

"And do you remember what you did about it?"

"I lost weight," she answered defiantly. "I changed my eating habits. I started exercising, and I felt a lot better."

I shook my head. "You thought about doing that, but you knew you'd get too tired and too busy to keep up with it. You took the other option. You got another job."

"I did *not!*" she yelled. Her voice was shrill. "I didn't quit. I *never* quit."

"You did this time. You decided you'd earned the right to quit, just this once."

She didn't know what to say to that. She looked around the apartment again, and the afterimage of my old place faded from the corners of my vision, leaving the bare carpet, the plastic, and the scribbled walls.

She dropped the bat. I could see her eyes filling up with tears.

"Why are you here?" she said. "What do you want?"

"I want you back. The new job's dull. There are a million things I could do in that office if I had the ambition, but I don't without you."

She laughed, wiping her eyes on a pajama sleeve. "So, you make changes in your new job. Your new boss sees how great you are and starts to depend on you. You work longer hours because you don't want to disappoint her, and then we're back where we started, except at a lower salary. I don't think so."

She shrugged her shoulders, and her pajamas changed to the pinstripes I'd seen her wearing at the airport. Her hair bounced from my usual sleep-tossed do into a classy style, and make-up appeared on her face. "You'd never be happy if you had me back. You'd always be trying to do your job better and faster, and eventually, you'd burn out again. Then, you'd get another job and start all over."

She was right.

"So what do we do?" I asked.

Her backpack — my backpack — materialized next to her feet. She picked it up and slung it over her shoulder in a gesture I knew well. "You are going to sneak out of here — quietly. The credit cards will give you enough problems without getting arrested for trespassing on top of it."

"How do you know about the credit cards?"

She looked up from adjusting her strap. "I know a lot of things now. I'm sorry about that, by the way. I was just — trying to get back. I was trying to get *me* back."

"No problem," I said. "I'll take care of it."

"I think you'll take care of it just fine." She finished adjusting the strap on her backpack and started for the door.

"Where are you going?" I said.

She stopped at the door and smiled. "To the airport."

I shook my head, flabbergasted. "And then what? Hop a plane?"

She looked at me pityingly. "You don't know anything, do you? I can only be in places where I lived. The office is out. There will be new tenants in here eventually. The airport is the only place left."

"You are going to haunt — O'Hare?" The idea sounded as ridiculous out loud as it did in my head.

"Sure. O'Hare doesn't have a ghost that I know of. I think it's high time it did, and I'm perfect for the job."

I stood there, blinking at her. "But — but —"

"Yes?" she had one hand on the doorknob, ready to leave.

"But what about me?" I said finally. "What am I going to do?"

She smiled again, that easy relaxed smile I'd been seeing in the mirror for a few months now. "Just what you've been doing."

And then she was gone. Without opening the door or even fading through it, she just vanished.

It took two years to get my credit straightened out. In the meantime, I lost a little more weight and found time to do silly things like style my hair before work.

I like it.

I like everything about my new life, including the fact that I can leave work at 5 PM without that nagging voice telling me to stay for just 5 more minutes — and then 5 minutes more . . .

I smile when I hear stories about the ghost of O'Hare. I smile because I know she loves the recognition, though she never performs for camera crews trying to catch her on film. I smile because I'm sure she's the best ghost in the world. She has to be.

Without the distractions of living, she can devote her whole self to being the best as what she does. I know that makes her happy, and I'm glad. I'm glad for both of us.   Ω

          THE GHOST OF ME

OOPS!

by Batya Swift Yasgur & Barry N. Malzberg

At first it was a tiny, tiny violation: he switched on the light on Sabbath. Of course, the law against using electricity was a subcategory of a more major law — the prohibition against lighting a fire — so said the Rabbis. But Rabbinic *pilpul* and hairsplitting aside, come on, how heinous could a simple light switch be? Innocuous, surely.

Rosenstein felt that he understood the innocuous. It had always been his outstanding gift.

So he flicked the switch. Oops! he said, in case the Almighty got the wrong idea. He could always claim a mistake. Sorry God, force of habit you know, I thought it was Tuesday.

But the switch did its job. Let there be light, and there was light.

Rosenstein waited. Waited for Divine retribution, for the thunder of cosmic disapproval, the lightning of punishment, obliterating this newfound light of liberation.

And waited.

No problem.

Nothing.

So Rosenstein, newly divorced on grounds of religious differences and thriving, he liked to think, within this new circumstance of flight and potential, became more daring. Recovering his religious roots by tearing them out of the ground, that was the idea. So: could he drive on Sabbath? Turn on the stove? Write a letter? Mow the lawn? More and more, tiny increments at first, gathering speed and momentum, until he was dancing to music in his living room. (Another Sabbath *verboten*).

Free, free of Rabbinic dicta, of Mom sitting, hushed and reverent in Synagogue, listening to today's Torah reading — the Ten Commandments. Free of Dad fingering his tallis and muttering of his inconstant son, free of his Orthodox wife and her grim predictions of his spiritual demise for outrageous religious viewpoints, free of Rabbis, Parchment and Penitence. Rosenstein danced as Miriam the prophetrice, sister of Moses, had danced with timbrel and cymbals, to celebrate the redemption from Egypt, as the pro-

prietors of the Golden Calf had danced before Moses. Dance of liberation.

Next step, then.

Well, what if he ate *tref* on a weekday? What if he ate *tref* on the Sabbath? What if —

What if he ate *tref* on Yom Kippur? In public, in the Norwegian Seaman's Seafood Diner, in the front window, his defiance open to all who would care to look within? The Rabbis and Hasidim of his youth, the dutifully religious ex-wife? To watch them shudder and squirm, like the very lobsters and shrimp in the cauldron of the briny sailor chef? What then?

Ah, such a question.

What else to do? The recently divorced but unregretfully apostosaic Rosenstein went out on Yom Kippur — the very next week — and did just that. Amongst a group of elderly, retired Norwegian boatmen in the Norwegian retreat on Atlantic Avenue, on the most holy day of the calendar. A forkful of shrimp, sip of creamed clam chowder, pat of butter on a roll. Not delicious — only in lustful rumors of the truly misbegotten was sin ecstasy — but certainly manageable, a sensation not unlike the relief he had felt when the light first blazed at his timid touch on the switch, and he had not been incinerated at that moment. He chewed heavily, swallowed, nodded at the retired seaman at the next table, pointed a fork at the *tref*. "Very good, nacht?" he said. "Nicht shrimp, guten?" Not Norwegian, probably, but foreign anyway, some kind of heavy, alien tongue — God's tongue perhaps (not Hebrew, as the Rabbis taught, nor Yiddish as the Hasidim insisted) — therefore approving, as God would not be.

Three owlish Hasidim at street level peered through the open window into the Norwegian Seaman's Seafood Diner, their faces radiating disapproval — or perhaps it was the heat of the late September afternoon.

Rosenstein winked at them, raising his fork and waving it ostentatiously. *"L'Chaim!"* he said loudly, the clamor of his apostasy like eighteen tiny legs clambering up the rope ladder toward freedom, toward the ship of rescue, "One must start somewhere, yes? After all, Norway was very kind to the Jews when Hitler knocked at the door."

The Hasidim glanced at each other. Solemn with the weight of consequential holiday, they gasped, shook their heads, and muttered something (in Yiddish) about getting to *shul* on time and praying for a lost soul. They hurried away, trailing shocked and sorrowful exclamations behind them.

Ha! Got them!

Rosenstein, triumphant, took another tiny shrimp and pounced upon it with his fork. The shrimp seemed to give a gleeful little squiggle as it accommodated itself to being speared. From surrounding tables, retired sailors grunted, sighed and semaphored. Rosenstein chewed, swallowed, and burped. A resounding belch, which wrenched the somnolent sailors out of their stupor. Oops! He had not planned on that. He definitely had not planned to burp.

But there it was; oops! — and the newly flatulated shrimp seemed to intersect with some tiny corridor of light within, churned, and was suddenly expelled with great speed and force. Shards of light, golden as a golden calf followed its trail of expulsion across the cafeteria. Rosenstein stared at the arcing shrimp with wonder.

Oops! Retired seamen cried out in astonishment. The expelled shrimp hit the window, bounced, grew sudden wings — little archangel's wings — swooped through an open space, disappeared into the flat Brooklyn terrain, and returned presently, somewhat enlarged, tugging a recalcitrant Hasid into the view of the amazed and spellbound Rosenstein. The Hasid looked annoyed, then horrified, the shrimp intent upon its act of transport. Rosenstein sought a roll to brandish, but the food had vanished, the room had darkened, the seamen had become a cluster of silence.

"Excess is not wisdom," whispered the shrimp, not only ambulatory but gifted with speech — non-Norwegian, non-Hebrew, non-Yiddish. "Rebellion is not affirmation, even a speaking shrimp is not victory."

Well, now. Indeed. Rosenstein transfixed, the Eleventh Commandment like a Hasid, like King Olaf himself, beating at the bars of his shore-bound heart:

THOU SHALT BE GENTLE IN THY DEFIANCE, HUMBLE IN ITS EXECUTION. Ω

FALL OF THE ENCHANTER: A PANTOUM

Tower fallen, the enchanter fled
Past the skulls piled into hills
Beside the river that now ran red
Power broken, beset with ills

Past the skulls piled into hills
Two crows watched with evil eye
Power broken, beset with ills
Even mages fall and die

Two crows watched with evil eye
Lances shatter and broadswords break
Even mages fall and die
What one holds, another can take

Lances shatter and broadswords break
Beside the river that now ran red
What one holds, another can take
Tower fallen, enchanter fled

— **Jon Hansen**

ORACLE

Sitting on the shelf of time,
Reading fortunes for a dime,
Oracle of fortunes told,
Sometimes written, always sold.

Dealing cards and casting stones,
Reading tea leaves, counting bones,
Gypsy lore it has been said,
Will cure ills, speak to the dead.

An ancient soul of legends born,
Haggard face shows time so worn,
Telling eyes that pierce and stare,
Seeing, knowing, so aware.

Sit before her for your fate,
Place some coins on rusty plate,
Oracle of fortunes told,
Sometimes spoken,
Always sold.

— **Jill Bauman**

by Jill Bauman

HEARTS AND MINDS

by Barbara Krasnoff

It's late in the afternoon, and I'm sitting around playing Hearts with Hirsch, Ruth, and Paolo on a rickety card table in front of a candy store, the type of which I haven't seen since I was about eight years old.

Hirsch is dealing out the cards while Paolo watches him with narrowed eyes. Paolo is sure that Hirsch cheats, but hasn't caught him at it yet. Ruth told me that she thinks Hirsch fakes cheating to drive Paolo crazy.

"So, Mark — what the fuck is a nice, middle-class boy like you doing here, anyway?" asks Hirsch, dealing me an ace of spades. He's a balding, fat guy who looks as if he should be smoking on a big cigar and screaming at his downtrodden sweatshop workers. Actually, he once headed up a major cell in the American Communist Party and got beaten up regularly trying to unionize Okies during the Depression. Go figure.

I look at him. "I got tired of dancing around with the other fags," I tell him. "You can only hang out in fabulous bars just so long before you get incredibly bored."

"Bullshit," says Ruth. She swings out of the candy store with a couple of bottles of Coke in one hand and a pack of cigarettes in the other, letting the screen door slam behind her. Today she is wearing a big-shouldered 1940s dress that makes her look like Lena Horne on a really good day. I've got to admit, that woman has style. "You never hung out at bars. Sugar, you probably had a monogamous relationship with a nice Jewish doctor and adopted 2.5 kids."

"Only one kid," I tell her. "And the nice Jewish doctor was actually a college professor."

"So," she says, lighting a cigarette thoughtfully, "why do you hang out around here so much? Not that we don't enjoy your company, but it's not like we have a lot in common."

"More than you'd think," I tell her. "A smashed head is a smashed head, whether you get it in Harlan County or at the Stonewall riots."

"Not true," says Hirsch, always ready for an argument. Excuse me — debate. "At Stonewall, you at least had reasonable access to media cover-

age, not to mention a lawyer. However, during the labor movement of the 1930s . . ."

"Shut up and play," Paolo grumbles. The guy couldn't have gotten much to eat when he was a kid; he's small, thin, and wiry. But mean. Really mean. Ruth once told me that he fought in several wars, in several countries. I've never had the nerve to ask him for any details.

Sunlight spills along the sidewalk and onto the brownstones across the street. I hear kids playing somewhere, so maybe it's after three P.M., but I don't know for sure. From inside the store, somebody puts the radio on and a clarinet starts to warble. Benny Goodman, I think. I'm normally not much for jazz — I like opera, and used to play La Boheme until Andrew, my otherwise patient Significant Other, threatened to break the CD player. But I've got to admit, the music does add to the atmosphere.

We trade cards across the table. Paolo throws out the two of clubs and stares accusingly at Hirsch, who smiles and tosses out an ace. The rest of us throw in our clubs, and the game begins.

After a couple of rounds, Hirsch grins and starts discarding spades. Ruth sucks on her cigarette calmly, unimpressed, while Paolo studies his hand with painful intensity. I play almost by instinct, not really caring if I win or lose. It's more fun to watch the others.

On the radio, Benny finishes his set, and Cab Calloway takes over with a slow, sensual riff on Minnie the Moocher. Ruth stubs out her cigarette. "I'm bored," she announces, and stands, grabbing my hand. "Come on, Mark, dance with me."

Paolo looks up from his hand. "In the middle of a game?"

She smiles at him. "The game can wait. Come on, honey, I need to move." And she does. I never liked to dance with Andrew — he had been a disco king in his youth, and I couldn't keep up — but with Ruth, all you have to do is shuffle your feet and sway your hips, and she does the rest.

Hirsch sits back and opens a Coke, while Paolo reaches under his chair for the Italian paper that he always keeps there and buries himself in it.

Around the second verse, Ruth starts to sing in a deep, almost tuneless voice, "She had a dream 'bout the King of Sweden. He gave her things that she was needin' . . ."

"You never dance with me like that," Hirsch complains, eyes firmly on her swaying rear.

"You want to dance like this?" Ruth asks. "Lose a few pounds."

Cab stops wailing, and Ruth gives me a firm kiss on the forehead. "Not bad," she tells me, and I happily take her hand for the next number when a voice says, "Excuse me?"

Somebody shuts off the radio with a click. We all turn and look. A young man is standing a few feet away, clutching a piece of paper in both hands and looking somewhat embarrassed, as though he just walked in on a bedroom scene. He's a kid, really, no more than 18 or 19. Neat blue suit, perfectly knotted tie, white shirt. Shoes so bright you could see up a nun's skirts. Short blond hair, a round, clean-shaven face —assuming he needs to shave — and a pair of shoulders that makes me want to grab him and run.

"Hi, gorgeous," I say. "New in town?"

The kid reddens, and hastily looks down at the piece of paper. "Ex — um — excuse me," he stammers. "I'm looking for, uh . . ."

"Spit it out," says Hirsch, amused. "We won't bite."

The kid takes a breath. "My name is Joseph Beckman," he says. "I have, right here . . ." and he fishes in his jacket pocket until he produces a small business card, which he hands across the table to Ruth.

"Joseph Beckman," she reads. "Assistant Shepherd, Church of Good News."

"Religious crap," Paolo mutters. The kid pulls himself up indignantly and starts to say something, but Ruth shakes her head at him.

"Ignore him," she advises. "He's just being obnoxious. Why don't you just tell us what you want?"

"I'm looking," says Joseph, "for a Mr. Samuel Hirsch."

Everyone looks at Hirsch, who shrugs. "That's me. Nu?"

Joseph puts out a hand. "I'm very glad to meet you, Mr. Hirsch. I have a wonderful gift for you. You have been baptized by proxy into the Church of Good News so that you may enter into the glory of His love."

Hirsch ignores the outstretched arm and bares his teeth at the kid in something that resembles a smile as interpreted by a shark. "Excuse me?" he asks softly.

"It's true," Joseph continues, pulling back his hand and ignoring — or not recognizing — the implicit threat. "In order to ensure that all souls have the chance to enter the Heavenly Kingdom, including those who may have not have accepted the Word, we enable them to be baptized by proxy. In this case, your son . . ."

"My son?" Hirsch shakes his head firmly. "You mean Sidney? The last I knew, the little weasel was married and living in Chicago."

Joseph looks a bit taken aback by this show of fatherly disaffection, but plows on gamely. "Well, about four years ago your son moved to Salt Lake City, where he is doing quite well. He is the father of three lovely children, a prosperous business owner . . ."

Hirsch's face is starting to get red. "A business owner, huh? I always knew he'd end up no good. Probably pays minimum wage, the little shit."

". . . a member of good standing of his church . . ."

Suddenly Paolo slams down his paper, stands, and points one finger firmly at Joseph. "Boy, you do not understand. The purveyors of false spirituality have brainwashed this man's son into adopting a sugar-coated hierarchical belief system and have persuaded him to kidnap his wife and children and move them to the heart of the fascist religious oligarchy. Thus, instead of carrying on the fight against the anti-democratic forces in the American government, he will be wearing the uniforms of the capitalist forces and press his innocent offspring into the mold of American McCarthyism. He has betrayed his family and his class."

There is a moment of respectful silence.

"Nicely put," says Ruth.

"A real ball-buster," approves Hirsch. "You ever speak in Union Square?"

"What they said," I tell him. "But you forgot to include the assumption of heterosexual privilege."

I look at Ruth, and add, "*White* heterosexual privilege." She grins at me.

Paolo shrugs. "Next time," he says, sits, and picks up his paper again.

The boy clears his throat. "Yes. Well, since your son has, through the good offices of the church, enabled you to join us . . ."

Hirsch's eyes narrow. "Kid, does it look as if, on my worst day, I'd want to join your Church of whatever?"

"The Church of Good News," the boy says patiently. "And if you just beheld the beauty . . ."

Hirsch pushes himself up from the table and takes a step toward the kid, who prudently retreats. "Listen to me, you miserable gonif, you stealer of souls," he growls. "If my son, may his name be wiped from the face of the earth, chooses to join your miserable institution and spend the rest of his life kissing the feet of a murderous god, I can't do anything about it. But I will not — I repeat, will not — accept any responsibility for his actions. Nor will I have anything to do with you, or him, now or in the future. Do you understand me?"

Joseph, who has more backbone than I gave him credit for, stands his ground. "Please reconsider. You don't know how joyous it is to spend eternity with the saved."

I take a step forward, meaning to get between Hirsch and this maniac, but Ruth puts a hand on my arm. "Don't worry," she whispers. "It's okay."

In fact, Hirsch has gone quiet. From where I stand, dangerously quiet. "Son," he says, almost gently. "Don't you think you'd better leave before somebody gets hurt?"

The kid looks at him, baffled. "But, don't you know? I mean . . . You can't hurt me. I'm . . . you're . . . we're . . . dead."

Silence. Hirsch stares back at the kid for a moment. Then he takes a deep breath, sits down, and grabs his cards. "Well," he says to the rest, "Are we playing Hearts, or not?"

Paolo throws down his paper and picks up his hand. "About time," he says. "Ruth, Mark, you in or out?"

Ruth shrugs, and lights another cigarette. The radio goes on again, and Woody Guthrie starts to sing about a union maid who never was afraid. Joseph is still standing there, looking totally confused, so I put a fatherly hand over his shoulders, and walk him away from the table. "They won't talk to you any more," I tell him. "You see, you really shouldn't have mentioned the 'D' word. They're a bit sensitive on the subject."

The boy shakes his head. "I don't understand," he says. "Why wouldn't they want to enter the Heavenly Kingdom rather than languishing here in this urban Purgatory deprived of the grace of Our Lord?"

I smile. "I'm sure it's very nice where you are," I tell him. "But the thing is — they're atheists. They don't believe in an afterlife." I shake his hand, and go back to the card game.   Ω

ESCAPE

The door may be inside a wardrobe,
Or you might slip right through a mirror.
You feel the tug of the Siren's song
And know you are its only hearer.

You may be pulled into a painting,
Find a rip in reality's seams.
Anything to get away from here
To a place you've seen only in dreams.

This world alone is not quite enough,
With its mysteries all unraveled.
You long for the call of Avalon,
To discover the road less traveled.

There are those who do not understand,
Saying, "Pull your nose out of those books —
None of it's true — you're wasting your time,"
With their indulgent or baffled looks.

Then you remember what Tolkien said
About prisoners pining and pale —
That only a jailer does not want
Any talk of escaping the jail.

So you slide through the wrinkle in time;
You return with a wind in the door.
The White Stag you follow leads you back
To your own mundane birthplace once more.

Yet now you have magic in your eyes:
Penumbra of glory lingers on,
Revealing ghosts in every street,
Elysian Fields in every lawn.

— Nicholas Ozment

A PAGEFUL OF CURSES
by Bruce Boston

CURSE OF THE GIANTESS'S HUSBAND

Stuffed Cornish game hens.
Spareribs by the bucket.
Double chocolate shakes.
Bag after bag of chips

gobbed with melted cheese.
Throughout each day and
long into the evenings
she sits wedged in her

favorite armchair watching
television and devouring.
With vertiginous abandon
gluttony and sloth scale

formerly unimagined heights.
Between "snacks" she dozes,
her gargantuan inhalations
and cacophonous snorts

drowning out car chases
and commercial breaks.
And as her mass mushrooms
his seems to shrink in kind.

No matter how hard he clings
to the edge of the mattress
before surrendering to sleep,
by daybreak he has tumbled

down the steeply inclined plane
of their Brodingnagian bed,
a pebble lodged at the base
of her mountainous rise.

CURSE OF THE UNREAL COUPLE

He is drawn to her emptiness,
Her negative enchantment.

Just as she is drawn
To the absence of him.

Finding nothing to embrace,
They beat on their chamber walls:

A sound that no one hears
Who is substantial.

CURSE OF THE WITCH'S HUSBAND

She only turns
him into a toad
two or three
times each week.

Not so bad in itself
being a toad,
except that toads
have to eat.

Mayflies are the worst,
their wings beating
all the way
down his throat.

CURSE OF THE SIREN'S SUITORS

When she sings they listen in rapture,
not so much to her words but her voice,
a voice that contains all manner of things:
dregs, dreams, delights, and darkling promises,
a distillation of what they would possess.

When they cross the water with eager hands
upon the oars, backs stretched, arms wide
against the waves, eyes open and gleaming,
they listen in rapture not so much to the
songs she sings as to how she sings them,

not to the words but what her voice portrays.
They listen in rapture as the hull shatters
and the masts crack and they dash their
bodies upon the rocks of her cave.

SHORE OF NIGHT, SHORE OF DAY

by Katrien Rutten

illustrated by Allen Koszowski

When Herek came home after a long day of mending nets, he found a stranger in his late wife's chair. She sat warming her stocking feet at the stove, her rich red skirts spread out around her; and she did not get up as he came in. A little black-and-white pig rooted about beneath the table.

Herek shut the door, drawing the bolts above and below, and looked at Gesim for an explanation. To his annoyance, his son shrugged and looked quickly away, then knelt to open the little stove door and began to build up the fire with elaborate care.

"Good day then, lady," said Herek with resignation, sitting down opposite her. "I suppose you are lost?" He noted with disapproval that she had set her boots beside the stove to dry — the surest way to ruin good leather.

"I think not," the stranger said. "Not if you are Herek, and if this is the ninth house on the Shore of Night." Her voice was strangely accented, and there seemed to be a smile hiding in it somewhere.

Herek frowned. "Who are you, and how come you here? Where are your servants?"

"I am called Sora," she said. "I walked here from Middell, leaving my escort there. To Middell I came from the Great Library of Barradil, in ten days' riding."

Herek sucked in his breath. The traders he knew reckoned at least twelve days to reach the gates of Barradil, even in good weather, and there was ice upon the roads.

"Why the haste?" he asked. "And who gave you my name?"

"At your neighbors' doors I came knocking," Sora said. "I asked them whose boat it was that I saw lying ready at the tide-edge, instead of hull up on a drying rack. Yours, they told me. When they asked why I wanted to know, I said that I wished to hire you. A midnight jaunt, said I, to my lover's house on Pennan Isle."

Just as Herek drew in breath to speak, she added, "But that is not why I am here."

Herek shifted upon his chair — he wanted to stretch his legs, but the lady's boots and the lady's pig were in the way. He scowled at Gesim, who had shed all pretense of not listening and sat motionless at Sora's feet with the poker still in his hand, looking up at her through his long lashes.

Deciding that he might get better answers with only one question at a time, Herek asked "Why are you here, then?"

"Ten days ago, the news came that my love is dead," Sora said. The smile had left her voice, and she drew her feet in beneath her skirts.

"What was his name?" Herek asked.

"Dimil. He was reported dead by those few who came back from the battle at Merrow Pass. They told me they'd seen Dimil fall, but they didn't find his corpse. Cowards! I don't think they ever looked for him, they were too busy running for their lives."

She sighed and stared past Herek's shoulder. Then her gaze returned to him. "I must know if he is truly dead."

"I'm sorry for your loss, lady," Herek said, scratching his beard. "But I've never heard of your Dimil, and there is nothing I can do to help you. You're the first stranger in Night since the year twenty-three."

A silence fell. She was still looking at him, her head tilted to one side like a bird's. Herek crossed his arms. He did not look away, but he made the witchsign with his left hand, hidden in the crook of his right elbow. The silence between them stretched like taffy while Gesim looked from the one to the other, apparently unaffected.

"I wonder," she said at last. Herek let out his breath silently.

"In the scrolls of the Great Library I found a certain skipping-song," Sora went on. "Have you not heard it?"

Herek stared at her, the hard fish-eyed stare that was his last resort against Gesim at his most recalcitrant. It did not seem to disconcert Sora in the least. In a low, lilting voice she sang:

"Where do they go? Far away,
"From the Shore of Night to the Shore of Day.
"When do they go? Turn about,
"When the moon is full and the tide is out.
"Where do they go then? I can't say,
"Where they go no live man may."

"I know that you take this month's dead to the Shore tonight," she added, "and I must go with you. If Dimil is dead, his shade will be there."

Gesim dropped the poker.

Sora smiled.

"Go to t'other room," Herek said softly, catching Gesim's eyes.

Somewhat to his surprise, his son rose immediately and fled the room without so much as a backwards glance at their visitor.

"You came here on the strength of a rhyme to tell me this?" Herek's voice sounded loud in the small room. "This gaffer's tale? I aim to do nothing this night, lady, other than take my ease and perhaps mend a shirt or two."

"A rhyme can be as strong as a rope, when other threads are woven in," said Sora. "Your son gave the game away." She stood up. "I know you will go. All that is left to discuss is your payment."

"Payment?" Herek echoed before he could stop himself.

"I would not expect you to take me along for nothing. And Gesim will need a bride-price someday, I dare say."

Sora reached into the depths of her left sleeve and drew out what looked like a lump of old honey. Then she spread her hands, and the honey uncoiled into a rope of amber beads. "That should satisfy all but the choosiest brides."

Herek nodded; his throat was too dry to speak. On feast days, his neighbor Rannis wore an amber amulet that had been in his family for generations. A Middell gem dealer had once offered Rannis a sum for it that equaled a full year's haul of fish. Every single bead in the necklace Sora held out to him was the size of Rannis' amulet.

And only last week, Gesim had strenuously denied all rumors of his dalliance with the tax-man's daughter.

Herek swallowed.

The tide was almost fully out. As Herek and Sora walked toward the solitary skinboat that lay near the tide-edge, the pig lagging at their heels, they crossed a banding of razor-shells that crackled underfoot. Herek saw Sora look about her with barely hidden fascination. He had lent her

Tannet's longcoat, and it was odd to see that familiar coat flapping at his side, when the face and stride were so different and not so infinitely dear.

Herek took hold of the woven handle fastened to the skinboat's prow and began to drag the boat toward the surf. Sora reached out a hand as if to help, then stopped herself. Herek didn't really need her help in any case: the skinboat was just that, merskin stretched out over wooden ribs and tied to a long runner on either side. One man could paddle or drag it with ease, although it could carry as many as thirty. The skinboat's shape veered out from a high narrow prow to a broad middle, designed to hold a large load of fish picked from the standing nets in the bay.

Every few months, when it was Herek's turn to make the crossing, the skinboat held another cargo. There was no sign of that cargo yet; beside Sora and himself, the beach was empty. Herek gestured to the skinboat that now lay bobbing on the waves. "You'd best get in first. Otherwise you'd have to walk through the dead, and that's not pleasant."

For the first time, Sora looked somewhat disconcerted. "But — are they here, then?" she asked, looking round. "Are you the only one who can see them?"

"No, and no," Herek said. "Here, take my hand, and step into the boat. Careful — place your feet in the middle, one on either side of the spine. If you stand on one side or lean too hard, the boat will go over."

It was odd, giving such instructions to a grown woman. But it was plain that they were needed — Sora had probably never been in a boat before. She acquitted herself very well, only dampening the hem of her skirts as she manoeuvered herself into the boat. Herek handed the pig in after her at her commanding look, sighing as he did so. Pigs were for eating, not for carrying about and cosseting.

"There. You'd best sit on the front bench." She walked forward gingerly and sat down where he pointed, at the far end of the boat.

Herek drew out the small slug-horn from under his shirt, took a deep breath, and set it to his lips, producing a sound both fierce and mournful.

He heard Sora gasp, but did not turn.

The dead were all around them. Men and women, old and young, naked and clad, but all grey, all staring. They drifted about without purpose, it seemed, but they drew ever closer to the skinboat and the surf.

Herek stood his ground, although the cold struck him like a fist as always.

"Come," he said. "You can't cross without me. Come."

They came. They fled into the skinboat in droves, in battalions, leaving no space uncovered but the bench where Sora sat. They parted around her like a river.

When the beach was empty once more, Herek stepped into the boat, which was too heavy now to rock under him, and took hold of his long paddle. Sora sat facing him, surrounded by the shades that were like a grey mist between them.

"Wait till we're past the surf and the nets," he said. "Then you can look for your Dimil."

Sora nodded and drew the longcoat closely about her. She was shivering. Herek did not think it was with fear, but rather with the cold that the dead brought with them.

Herek shifted on the hard bench. Sora had been calling her love for what felt like hours, now. They were not even halfway yet — he looked up at the stars and made a broad stroke with his paddle, steering them slightly to the left — and already he was tired, his shoulders still cramped from his day's work on the nets.

"Dimil!" Sora's voice now sounded more than a little impatient.

Herek sighed.

Tannet had come to him right away, on the first full moon after her death. It had been Uff's turn to make the crossing that night, but Uff had ceded to him, as was the custom when one of their own stood waiting on the shore.

Tannet waited beside the skinboat as he called the other dead. She didn't have that sightless stare most of the others had, and he could almost believe that she looked kindly upon him. When Herek shoved off, she sat down beside him, her ghostly form hovering above the bench. She was cold, of course, and she could not hear him or speak to him; but she was there beside him, and in the midst of his blank sorrow he'd been glad.

Sora breathed in sharply, and Herek looked up.

She was standing in the prow, carefully balanced, hemmed in by the dead on all sides except one. Pressed up between Sora and the right top runner was a single shade.

"I found him," Sora whispered. "It's Dimil." Her tone was jubilant. "Dimil, can you hear me?"

"The dead can't hear, lady," Herek said as gently as he could. He was sorry, now, that he had taken her offer. What had she expected, that she should look so pleased? Her lover was dead, and there would be no fond last words exchanged between them.

Sora did not appear to listen. Instead, she bent down to where the pig bustled about her feet, and picked it up by the scruff of its neck. Then she moved her other hand, and something glinted. A thin stripe marked the pig's throat as Sora's hand stroked it. Then the blood gushed out, steaming, and the pig began to wail like a baby.

Sora stashed the small knife in her sleeve. Her face was white as bone.

"Dimil," she said, and the shade turned its dark head. "Dimil, I bind you! All be bound!"

Slowly, the tall shade bent forward, wavering, and sank to its knees.

Herek became aware that he could not move. His arms and legs ached with the strain of trying to answer his summons. It seemed that he, at least, was well and truly bound.

Sora sat down upon her bench, still facing Herek, Dimil's shade kneeling between them.

"Why did you leave me?" she said.

Dimil gave no answer other than a long gusting sigh.

"I bind you to speak and hear," Sora said, speaking the words with great care. "I found you; I bound you; I shed red blood for you. Why did you leave me?"

"I never left you," Dimil said slowly.

Herek shivered. The voice of a dead man should not sound so young, so lost. He wondered whether Dimil's shade would ever reach the Shore at all, now that Sora had given it life enough to speak.

"You went off to war and got yourself killed!" Sora said.

Dimil shook his head. "Not to spite you, love. I thought you were proud. . . ." His slow, halting speech trailed off, and he gave another sigh.

Sora cast down her eyes. "I was proud," she whispered, "until I knew the cost."

Dimil moved his hand as though to lay it on her shoulder; but then Sora looked up, her gaze as fierce now as a young harrier's.

"Stay," she said. "Don't leave me. I know how to work it so you can stay."

Dimil did not move. "Why?" he said at last.

Sora looked as though she were about to stomp her feet with anger. Herek hoped she wouldn't; the skinboat's hide was tough, but not made to withstand that kind of treatment.

"Don't you want to live?" Sora said. "Don't you

want to walk in the sun again? To be with me? I can't believe you'd want to stay a thing of smoke, blown about on the wind!" She waved her hands as she spoke, and her right hand carved a path through Dimil's stomach.

"Oh!" Sora snatched her hand back, looking stricken. "I'm sorry," she said, her eyes still on the ragged hole.

Dimil appeared to take no notice. His empty gaze was fixed not on Sora, but on the sea behind her and the faint glimmer appearing on the horizon.

"I won't let you go!" Sora said. "I will give you time, whether you want it or no." There was a fey look to her as she drew forth the knife again.

Herek gripped his paddle. The puddle of pig's blood on the bottom of the skinboat had begun to mix with the bilgewater, and he could feel the use of his limbs returning. He was determined to knock Sora over with his paddle rather than let her turn the knife on herself. Herek was quite surprised when she lunged towards him, instead. She had to step forward to reach him, and that gave him the time to throw himself aside. But there was little room at the narrow end of the boat, and the knife aimed at his heart sliced into his right arm. Sora drew back to strike again. Herek swiftly brought the paddle down over her wrist.

Sora cried out, and the knife clattered against the bench and fell behind it. Herek bent swiftly to pick it up and stow it in his belt.

"No more of that, if you please," he said, sitting down again. He was feeling very tired, and his arm hurt.

Sora stared at him, panting, and then turned back to Dimil. "He's bleeding. Can you see?" she said.

"Yes," Dimil said reluctantly. "The only color. Everything else is grey."

"Move, then," Sora said. "You can slip in there, where his life is running out."

Dimil did not move, although a shiver went through his form.

"I saw my friends die at Merrow Pass," he said. "Dying hurt . . . less than that did. They are here. Now." Sora flicked her gaze towards the shades crowded about her, then looked back at Dimil, frowning. "I want to go with them," he said. "Not stay here on . . . borrowed time."

Dimil sagged against the top runner. Herek felt underneath the bench, found a bit of rag and tied it around his arm, staunching the runnel of blood.

Sora pressed her fist to her mouth, looking now at Herek, now at the silent shade of her lover.

"Sit down," Herek said. "We're losing moonlight. We need to press on if we're to get your Dimil to the Shore in time."

She obeyed him. Herek began to paddle again, long sure strokes. The movement pulled at the gash in his right arm, but it felt good to be doing something familiar. The dead all around him, their cold sinking into his bones, their staring eyes gleaming in the moonlight — all this was habitual and held no fear for him. But the woman on the other bench was a terror and a mystery.

As they neared the elusive glimmer of the Shore of Day, Herek saw Dimil's shade slip away to the middle of the boat and lose his shape there, merging with the host of the dead. Sora made no move to stop him: she sat silently on the bench, her shoulders hunched with exhaustion.

Herek paddled steadily. The Shore shone brightly now, the moon a blazing beacon above it.

As always, the skinboat seemed to grow lighter as it neared the Shore, and the dead took on a less forbidding aspect, glimmering now at the edges like simmerweed.

Sand scraped at the bottom of the skinboat, and Herek looked up and squinted against the glare. They had reached the Shore. Already the dead were moving, flowing with single-minded purpose towards the blazing sand. He felt them pass him by in wave upon wave of cold. In a handful of breaths, all the dead were upon the Shore, dispersing, moving into the blinding light with joyful speed. None looked back; none halted.

The skinboat rocked as Sora stood up unsteadily. Herek, alarmed, stuck his paddle into the sand to steady the empty boat. "Sora, sit down!" he called. "We must go back. This is no place for the living."

Sora said nothing: her back was turned to him, her hands gripping the top runner. Then she leaned forward and slung herself overboard. The sandy bottom was only a foot below, but Herek lunged forward as the boat rocked beneath him, abandoning his paddle. "Sora, don't!"

Sora stood beside the boat a moment, then slowly walked forward through the surf, toward the Shore and the receding dead. "Dimil!" she called, and set foot upon the Shore.

Her foot found no purchase upon the sand; it fell through, and seawater fountained upwards from the hole she had made. Sora floundered and put out a hand to steady herself. Herek saw her balance fail, saw her fall to the side, and flung himself across the prow, hooking his feet under the front bench.

He caught her right shoulder, and she turned in his grip — but toward him, not away. "Grab hold of the prow," he said, guiding her hands to it. Sora obeyed him, although her eyes were as empty as those of the dead. Herek braced himself and took hold of her wrists. "Push off with your feet." He had no idea whether she touched bottom or not.

Sora rose slightly upon a wave, and he hoisted her up onto the prow by the wrists and then by the back of her longcoat.

There she lay, spent, as he pushed off and slowly turned the skinboat into the waves, turning his back upon the Shore.

When they were well underway, Herek grabbed her shoulders and pulled her down into the boat, settling her awkwardly with her back against the bench. Still she would not speak, although she followed him with her gaze as he sat back down and began to paddle.

She looked like a bird that had outflown its reach, spent itself and plummeted towards a meagre perch on a bit of rock, reduced to holding on and holding on only.

The way back seemed much longer, as always, even though the boat had shed its load.

The Shore of Night loomed darkly before them when Sora rose from her seat. Herek watched her make her way toward him, crouching to maintain her balance. She only stumbled once.

Sora sat down to his left, leaving a foot or so of bench between them to give him room to paddle. Seawater still dripped slowly from her skirts, and she bent down to wring them. "Your wife is dead, I'm told," she said, wringing industriously.

Herek turned his head to look at her, but said nothing.

"Did you take her across, after she died?"

Herek nodded and steered the boat closer into

the wind. "She sat beside me," he said slowly, remembering. "She laid her hand atop mine — not touching, of course. And when we touched Shore, she was the last to leave. But she never spoke, or looked at me."

Sora nodded. "You must think me a fool," she said, looking out over the choppy waves. "I daresay none of your folk ever tried to halt the dead or bind them into the living."

"Well, no," Herek mused. "But then we never had the trick of it; or if we did, we forgot it long ago."

Sora's head whipped round. "Really?" she whispered. "And what will you do, now that you know?"

Herek pulled his paddle through the water with great force; his right hand and wrist were dripping wet, and he could feel the sting of the spray in the wound on his upper arm. "Nothing," he said at last.

He looked at Sora. She bit her lip, and said nothing.

"But if you had shown me your secret ere my wife died, I might give you another answer."

They watched the sky slowly lighten in the east, the only sound the splashing of Herek's paddle.

"It was brave, what you did," Herek said then. "Not many would dare set foot upon the Shore of Day. Not many would dare bribe the ferryman, either."

Sora laughed. It wasn't her best laugh, Herek guessed; but it was a good effort. "You surprise me. I would think that you'd be swamped with supplicants."

Herek snorted. "T'other folk hereabouts are well aware of our legend, though it's not some-

thing they'd speak of to a stranger. But when we bring our fish to market in Middell, we have to use go-betweens to get a good price. No one will stand us a drink to seal the bargain; no one will give us a word or a nod if they can avoid it. Our daughters are not sought after, and if a son of ours wants to marry, he pays the bride-gift four times over."

"Now I understand why you took the amber," Sora said. "From the look of you when you came in, I thought you'd throw it in my face. But why do they treat you so? What you do is surely a blessing and a boon, both to the dead and the living."

Herek scratched his beard. "That's — a pleasant view of things, but not many share it hereabouts."

Sora looked down. "I hope you will be here, or your son, when I come to the Shore of Night, to take me across the water," she said. "It comforts me to think so."

Herek swallowed and said nothing as she laid her hand on his.

Together, they watched the sun come up over the Shore of Night.   Ω

TWO ILLUSTRATED LIMERICKS

I really don't like Uncle John.
His lousy taste just lingers on.
    But Ma says: "He's hot,
    And all that we've got.
Keep eating until he's all gone."

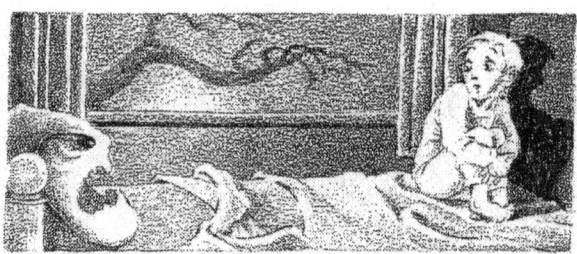

I'm waiting for dawn to arrive.
It's lighter now; it's almost five.
    My eyes are all blurred,
    But I haven't stirred.
I think that my pillow's alive.

— **George Barr**

by Katrien Rutten

TWO CENTS WORTH

by Alan Dean Foster

illustrated by David Grilla

It was April, and the heat was only unrelenting. By May and certainly by June it would become unbearable, and people would begin to die. The misery would persist until the monsoon arrived sometime in late June or early July, Knowles knew.

Not that it mattered to him. In a day or two he would be on a plane back to London, his business in Agra complete. Everything was going smoothly and he anticipated no roadblocks to closing the deal. The contract had been hard-won, of course. Any time you did business with Indians, it always was. That made the terms he had been able to extract all the more satisfying. One rose, he firmly believed, to the level of one's competition.

This morning's difficult, occasionally fractious discussion had left his throat drier than he had realized. Uncharacteristically, he had neglected to leave the meeting with a bottle of something cold and refreshing. Outside the steel and air-conditioned cocoon of the Mercedes, the great living sea that was Mother India heaved and surged around him. Camels and the great wooden disks that were the wheels of the single-axled carts they pulled slowed but did not stop traffic. Neatly dressed men, women, and sometimes children on buzzing motorbikes and scooters skittered in and out of the mass of traffic like angry waterbugs navigating a crowded swamp.

Three-wheeled powered rickshaws, mostly painted green and yellow, pocketa-pocketaed along on the sidelines, trying to get their passengers or cargo to their respective destinations while keeping out of everyone else's way. Astoundingly overloaded Tata and Ashok-Leyland trucks, not one of which would meet minimum safety standards in Europe or America, lumbered through the mass of traffic with saurupodian grace while engaged in a gruff, eternal ballet with ancient, wheezing busses not one of which could boast of glass in a single window.

Their weight distributed with Euclidian precision, a family of five balanced on a single motor scooter squeezed by on his right: father, mother, and three small kids. It was not a circus act; just classic Indian commuting. Idly, Knowles found himself imagining the mess they'd make if they were unlucky enough to encounter a speeding bus while cutting through an intersection. The bus would be unable or unwilling to stop, he knew. The family would go flying. There would be a flurry of recriminations, shouts, tears. Eventually, some municipal authorities would appear, as if out of nowhere, to clean it all up. And more than a billion people, one sixth of humanity, would get on with their lives.

He was still thirsty.

Knowles did not often act on impulse: certainly not in his business dealings. But a cold drink was a cold drink, so long as the bottle was properly sealed, and he was unwilling to wait until they reached the hotel. Leaning forward slightly, leather upholstery squeaking beneath the tailored tropical silk of his trousers, he murmured to the driver.

"I need a cold drink, Raju. Pull over someplace."

While startled by the request, the chauffeur did not look back at his important passenger. Though a poor man, he felt he enjoyed a fortunate life. To take one's eyes off traffic while driving in an Indian city was to invite suicide. "Here, sir?"

Amused by the man's response, Knowles glanced briefly to his right, out the tinted window. "Yes, here. Why not? The drinks for sale here come from the same plant as the ones at the hotel, don't they?"

"Yes sir. I suppose so, sir. Please, just let me find a good place."

"Any place will do. Any stand." Knowles leaned back into the cushioning seat. He was enjoying himself.

At least, he was until the driver finally settled on one of the hundreds of tiny clapboard streetside stands, most of which were smaller than the bathroom in the suite at the executive's hotel. Raju pulled over, got out, and opened the passenger-side door of the Mercedes. It was as if the man had opened the door to a commercial oven. But having made the suggestion, Knowles felt compelled to brazen it out.

Even though he did nothing more strenuous than get out of the car, he began perspiring immediately. He could feel the clammy droplets drip-dripping from his armpits down his sides. Well, he had intended to change as soon as he got back to the hotel anyway. A dip in the pool would fix everything.

The man behind the battered, splintered wooden plank that served as a counter front for the cubicle was slender and active. You expected both in India. Everyone was attuned to business as a way of life, and there were very, very few fat people. There was no sidewalk, of course. Where the cracked and abused asphalt layer of the street ended, dirt began. Cut by occasional rivulets and rills, what passed for the space between the road and the first tattered real buildings was paved only with garbage, rocks, and pieces of flaked roadbed. Even the plastic and paper litter looked hot.

Efficient and expectant, the cubicle keeper inquired of the driver as to his customers' needs. While the chauffeur ordered, the several locals who were hanging out looked up from their seats at one of the two tables that had been set out on the dirt and gazed at the tall European with unabashed interest. Such directness was another Indian trait. If they thought he spoke any Hindi, Knowles knew, within minutes they would openly be asking him the intimate details of his life; everything from did he have children to how much did he make in a year.

Raju came back with a pair of cool, if not cold, Fantas. While Knowles sipped his, after carefully wiping off the rim, he contemplated the endless parade of animals and humanity that overflowed the overworked street as thoroughly as floodwaters ever filled a riverbed. It parted only for a pair of Brahma cows.

Chewing their cuds while seated serenely in the middle of traffic, they ignored the lethal hysteria swirling all around them, secure in holy bovine confidence that everything from lurching cement trucks to rampaging interstate buses would swerve to miss them. And in truth, there was not so much as a scratch on hindquarter or flank. Of all the thousands of sacred steers Knowles had encountered on his many visits to the subcontinent, he had yet to see one that had been injured by a vehicle.

The beggar did not seem to step out of the human current so much as appear before him. He was of average height, about five foot six, and clad in dirty but intact cotton pants and overshirt. Stained as if by coal, his feet were unshod. Though uncut and hanging almost to his shoulders, his straight black hair had been given a cursory combing. The face was lean and undistinguished, the nose slightly hooked. Higher up, black eyes stared unblinkingly at Knowles. The mans right hand was extended toward him, palm open and facing up, in a pose familiar since time began.

Knowles ignored him. It was what you had to do, he felt. Giving the man money would only serve to immediatey draw a crowd, and the executive had not yet finished his drink. He turned slightly away. Not deliberately, but just enough to show he was uninterested.

The beggar stayed, hand out, eyes fixed, staring. The index finger rose. One rupee, the man was asking silently. About two cents at current exchange rates, Knowles knew. It didn't matter. It wasn't the money. It was the principle of the thing. The man looked healthy enough, especially compared to some pitiful specimens the executive had seen. Agra was a reasonably prosperous place. There was work to be had. Knowles believed it was his responsibility not to encourage the fellow.

At least he was being quiet about it. Nothing more aggressive than the politely upraised index finger. But the unbroken stare was becoming unnerving. Irritated now, Knowles turned further away and muttered, "Nahi, nahi."

The man could not or would not take the hint. He remained where and as he was silently, persistently demanding. While clearly uneasy, the chauffeur was reluctant to intervene. Not so the shopkeeper. Carrying the pan of soapy water with which he had been scrubbing his walls and few dishes, he came out from behind his makeshift counter and began yelling at the beggar. While Knowles could not follow the rapid stream of annoyed Hindi, it was clear enough what the shopkeeper was saying. Get lost, and quit bugging my customers.

The beggar ignored him, his unswerving, unbroken stare reserved solely for the well-dressed European. Knowles drank a little faster. The man was ruining the small pleasure of the cold drink.

There was a sudden loud, almost shocking splash as the shopkeeper heaved the filthy contents of the dishpan. The dirty water struck the beggar square in the face. For the first time, his eyes closed and he twitched slightly. Behind Knowles, the cruel laughter of the slightly better-off came from the men seated at the table. The beggar's black eyes opened and shut a couple of times as he blinked away the wastewater. Otherwise he hardly moved. Displaying either maniacal determination or immense natural dignity, he remained where he was, the arm still outstretched, never having wavered even when he had been struck by the water. The index finger remained upraised. One rupee. Two cents.

With the eyes of the now amused men at the table following him, Knowles handed the empty soda bottle to the chauffeur, who returned it to the still irritated shopkeeper. The executive let himself back into the car, careful not to burn his fingers on the door. As chilled air enveloped him and the car started to pull slowly back out onto the pavement, he saw the beggar outside the window. The man was bent over and staring in at him, expectant palm hovering outside the tinted glass. The beggar followed like that until the car accelerated slightly and entered traffic.

Knowles never looked back. His thoughts were already elsewhere. He had automatically put the encounter with the possibly deranged beggar out of his mind.

Within the grand lobby of the multi-story, five-star hotel, men and women of many nationalities promenaded freely. Sikhs sporting tightly wound, multi- colored turbans discussed business with visitors from opposite sides of the world while Indian women draped in sarees of brilliantly colored silk and gold thread flowed frictionlessly across thick woolen carpets from Tibet. Laughing and giggling, several innocent children of the privileged chased each other in the direction of the pool.

Knowles hesitated as he approached the gold-colored elevators. Work and the subsequent drive back to the hotel had made him hungry. Not hungry enough for a meal. A proper dinner was still hours away. But a quick snack would be nice.

The hotel boasted a fine bakery. Entering and finding himself alone, he scanned the contents of the wood and glass cases while waiting for the absent attendant to put in an appearance. The slick sugary sheen of freshly chilled Napoleons and dark chocolate eclairs was tempting enough, but he had learned from previous trips to develop a taste for the fine local sweets. He decided on a quarter kilo of small rectangles of dense pastry made with a dough of semolina flour and finely ground cashew nuts that had been sweetened with Lebanese honey and rose syrup.

Where was the attendant? Sensing slight movement behind him, he turned from inspecting the high-caloric contents of the display cases, and nearly stumbled with shock. Staring back at him was not the attendant, but the unblinking beggar who had accosted him outside the roadside stand.

Black eyes bored into the executive's own. The open palm extended toward him.

This was disgraceful, an outraged Knowles felt. There was no way on Earth such a vagabond ought to have been able to slip into the hotel past its intense and ever watchful security. Evidently a staff that was not always watchful, he decided angrily. He would have a few harsh words for the management, harsh words indeed!

"Nahi!" he barked furiously as he pushed past the man. Though the brief physical contact was rough, even challenging, the beggar did not respond, either with word or gesture. Instead, he simply turned and followed Knowles, tracking the executive with open palm and unblinking eyes.

When he was halfway to the elevators, Knowles turned to look back. To his relief, the beggar was gone. Not surprising, the executive decided. If the man had any sense at all, if he knew what was good for him, he would already have slipped out of the hotel by whatever mysterious way he had sneaked in. It was unconscionable to think such individuals could make their way into a hotel of this class. Perhaps the next time he visited Agra, Knowles decided, he would take his trade elsewhere.

He was debating whether to return to the bakery when the elevator arrived. The hell with it, he decided. He would order something from room service.

The latter was so prompt and so good and the waiter who brought it to the room so politely obsequious that Knowles magnanimously decided to forget the letter of complaint he had composed in his mind. A following swim and a fine dinner in the hotel's main restaurant settled him further into a state of general contentment. Tomorrow he would be off anyway, back to London, the contract signed to his satisfaction. He was looking forward

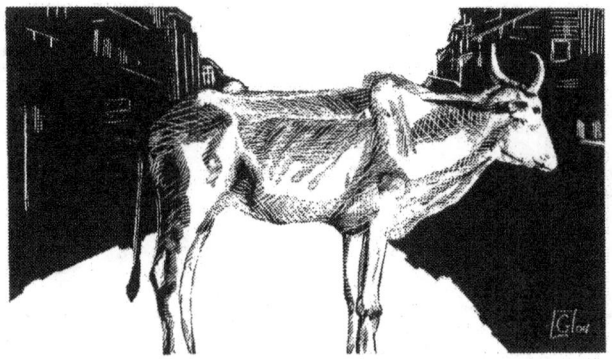

to escaping from the appalling heat and poverty and getting back to real civilization.

It was while coming out of the shower that he nearly bumped into the beggar.

Knowles was not a man easily frightened. He was used to commanding, to giving orders, and to having them obeyed. He was also physically much bigger than the lean whip of an obviously under-nourished intruder. The man was between him and the door. A second door accessed the hall from the sitting room of the suite. If he broke and ran for it, would this insane intruder chase him and try to stop him? A thought made the executive suddenly nervous. Was his unwanted visitor armed? Even beggars could afford a cheap knife.

But there was no threat in the man's open, staring eyes. Only a silent demanding reinforced by the open palm, the upraised index finger. One rupee. Damn the bastard! Knowles would not give in. It was a matter of principle. The letter of complaint he had intended to write to hotel management returned in full fury. Bad enough the transient had managed to sneak into the hotel. For him to find his way upstairs, to Knowles' very room, was inexcusable. Turning, he started for the sitting room.

The beggar moved to block his path.

For the first time, Knowles found himself growing slightly concerned. There was still no sign of a weapon, but who knew what a madman like this was capable of doing? Retreating slowly, never taking his eyes off the intruder, he contemplated picking up the phone and dialing security. Ordinarily, the gesture alone would be enough to frighten off any intruder. Any sane intruder, the executive reminded himself.

"Get out of here," he snapped as he backed away. Who knew what possibly contagious diseases lurked within those soiled cotton garments? Was the room already infected with something unseen? He felt the wall and window bump up behind him. Arm outstretched, the man continued to approach. True to form, he had still not uttered a word. A small piece of garbage from the dirty dishwater the shopkeeper had thrown in his face still clung to his left cheek.

Enough, Knowles decided. This was going to stop, and it was going to stop here and now. And if the hotel could not do its job, well, he would damn well have to do it for them. Balling his right hand into a tight fist, he drew back his arm.

And screamed as he felt the window vanish behind him.

by Alan Dean Foster

"He fell."

Sergeant Tarun and Inspector Aggrawal studied the place on the pale pavement near the pool where the body had been found. Only the slightest hint of a stain remained, the hotel staff having scrubbed furiously at the spot all morning. Fortunately, the accident had occurred late at night, after the pool area was closed. Only one hotel guest had been disturbed, and that was the unfortunate woman out for an early morning swim who had discovered the body. Her hysteria had been cured by a clearing of her bill.

"But what was he doing on the roof?" Tilting back his head, the Inspector squinted up at where the sharp crest of the hotel intersected the haze-filled pre-monsoon sky. It was going to be hot today. It was going to be hot until July.

"Who says he was on the roof?" Kneeling, the sergeant studied the place of demise. The chalk that had been used to outline the broken, splattered remains of the corpse had long since been scoured away by the hotel staff.

"He had to have been on the roof." The Inspector was as confident in person as he had been in his report. "All the windows in this hotel are sealed and can only be opened with a special key, in the event of emergency or a breakdown in the air con system."

Sergeant Tarun straightened. "I expect we'll never know exactly what happened."

The Inspector nodded thoughtfully. "At least we can be sure it wasn't robbery. He had two hundred pounds, a hundred Euros, and four or five thousand rupees in his room."

"Lot of good it does him now." The sergeant looked up at his superior. "Chai?"

Aggrawal nodded. Stopping on the way back to the station for the traditional small cup of tea and milk, they were intercepted by a beggar. The woman had a babe in arms and a toddler at her feet, one finger shoved up its dirty nose. It regarded them out of innocent dark eyes that showed a spirit of curiosity that had not yet been crushed by life. The Inspector handed her a coin. He always kept a handful of small change in his pocket for just such encounters.

Besides being right, it was the sensible thing to do. Ω

CEMETERY TOUR, MONTREAL, EARLY NOVEMBER 2001

So we made our little jokes
and took our pictures
in the rain and the gathering dark,
as the mausoleums,
like cramped, windowless houses,
stood in sullen silhouette
against the yellow leaves
and the orange glow of the city sky.

Maybe we grew a little less jolly
with the realization that there was real pain here,
that the ones who passed through these iron doors,
into these narrow houses, were still loved,
and even the pink lawn flamingos on one of the graves
didn't seem as funny anymore,
as the dead waited patiently for us to leave.

— Darrell Schweitzer

The Classic Horrors

I wrestled with the dead thing; it thrust itself upon me and forced me back.....
The Upper Berth
by F. Marion Crawford

by Allen Koszowski

THE UPPER BERTH

by F. Marion Crawford

illustrated by George Barr

Somebody asked for the cigars. We had talked long, and the conversation was beginning to languish; the tobacco smoke had got into the heavy curtains, the wine had got into those brains which were liable to become heavy, and it was already perfectly evident that, unless somebody did something to rouse our oppressed spirits, the meeting would soon come to its natural conclusion, and we, the guests, would speedily go home to bed, and most certainly to sleep. No one had said anything very remarkable; it may be that no one had anything very remarkable to say. Jones had given us every particular of his last hunting adventure in Yorkshire. Mr. Tompkins, of Boston, had explained at elaborate length those working principles, by the due and careful maintenance of which the Atchison, Topeka, and Santa Fé Railroad not only extended its territory, increased its departmental influence, and transported live stock without starving them to death before the day of actual delivery, but, also, had for years succeeded in deceiving those passengers who bought its tickets into the fallacious belief that the corporation aforesaid was really able to transport human life without destroying it. Signor Tombola had endeavoured to persuade us, by arguments which we took no trouble to oppose, that the unity of his country in no way resembled the average modern torpedo, carefully planned, constructed with all the skill of the greatest European arsenals, but, when constructed, destined to be directed by feeble hands into a region where it must undoubtedly explode, unseen, unfeared, and unheard,

into the illimitable wastes of political chaos. It is unnecessary to go into further details.

The conversation had assumed proportions which would have bored Prometheus on his rock, which would have driven Tantalus to distraction, and which would have impelled Ixion to seek relaxation in the simple but instructive dialogues of Herr Ollendorff, rather than submit to the greater evil of listening to our talk. We had sat at table for hours; we were bored, we were tired, and nobody showed signs of moving.

Somebody called for cigars. We all instinctively looked towards the speaker. Brisbane was a man of five-and-thirty years of age, and remarkable for those gifts which chiefly attract the attention of men. He was a strong man. The external proportions of his figure presented nothing extraordinary to the common eye, though his size was above the average. He was a little over six feet in height, and moderately broad in the shoulder; he did not appear to be stout, but, on the other hand, he was certainly not thin; his small head was supported by a strong and sinewy neck; his broad, muscular hands appeared to possess a peculiar skill in breaking walnuts without the assistance of the ordinary cracker, and, seeing him in profile, one could not help remarking the extraordinary breadth of his sleeves, and the unusual thickness of his chest. He was one of those men who are commonly spoken of among men as deceptive; that is to say, that though he looked exceedingly strong he was in reality very much stronger than he looked. Of his features I need say little. His head

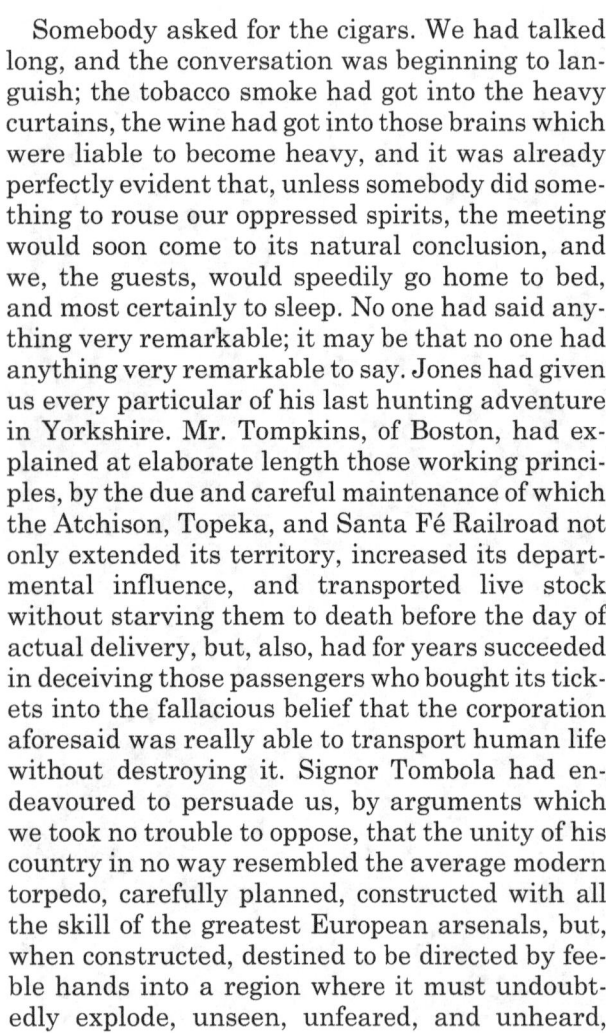

is small, his hair is thin, his eyes are blue, his nose is large, he has a small moustache, and a square jaw. Everybody knows Brisbane, and when he asked for a cigar everybody looked at him.

"It is a very singular thing," said Brisbane.

Everybody stopped talking. Brisbane's voice was not loud, but possessed a peculiar quality of penetrating general conversation, and cutting it like a knife. Everybody listened. Brisbane, perceiving that he had attracted their general attention, lit his cigar with great equanimity.

"It is very singular," he continued, "that thing about ghosts. People are always asking whether anybody has seen a ghost. I have."

"Bosh! What, you? You don't mean to say so, Brisbane? Well, for a man of his intelligence!"

A chorus of exclamations greeted Brisbane's remarkable statement. Everybody called for cigars, and Stubbs, the butler, suddenly appeared from the depths of nowhere with a fresh bottle of dry champagne. The situation was saved; Brisbane was going to tell a story.

"I am an old sailor," said Brisbane, "and as I have to cross the Atlantic pretty often, I have my favourites. Most men have their favourites. I have seen a man wait in a Broadway bar for three-quarters of an hour for a particular car which he liked. I believe the bar-keeper made at least one-third of his living by that man's preference. I have a habit of waiting for certain ships when I am obliged to cross that duck-pond. It may be a prejudice, but I was never cheated out of a good passage but once in my life. I remember it very well; it was a warm morning in June, and the Custom House officials, who were hanging about waiting for a steamer already on her way up from the Quarantine, presented a peculiarly hazy and thoughtful appearance. I had not much luggage — I never have. I mingled with the crowd of passengers, porters, and officious individuals in blue coats and brass buttons, who seemed to spring up like mushrooms from the deck of a moored steamer to obtrude their unnecessary services upon the independent passenger. I have often noticed with a certain interest the spontaneous evolution of these fellows. They are not there when you arrive; five minutes after the pilot has called 'Go ahead!' they, or at least their blue coats and brass buttons, have disappeared from deck and gangway as completely as though they had been consigned to that locker which tradition unanimously ascribes to Davy Jones. But, at the moment of starting, they are there, clean shaved, blue coated, and

ravenous for fees. I hastened on board. The Kamtschatka was one of my favourite ships. I say was, because she emphatically no longer is. I cannot conceive of any inducement which could entice me to make another voyage in her. Yes, I know what you are going to say. She is uncommonly clean in the run aft, she has enough bluffing off in the bows to keep her dry, and the lower berths are most of them double. She has a lot of advantages, but I won't cross in her again. Excuse the digression. I got on board. I hailed a steward, whose red nose and redder whiskers were equally familiar to me.

"One hundred and five, lower berth," said I, in the businesslike tone peculiar to men who think no more of crossing the Atlantic than taking a whisky cocktail at down-town Delmonico's.

The steward took my portmanteau, greatcoat, and rug. I shall never forget the expression on his face. Not that he turned pale. It is maintained by the most eminent divines that even miracles cannot change the course of nature. I have no hesitation in saying that he did not turn pale; but, from his expression, I judged that he was either about to shed tears, to sneeze, or to drop my portmanteau. As the latter contained two bottles of particularly fine old sherry presented to me for my voyage by my old friend Snigginson van Pickyns, I felt extremely nervous. But the steward did none of these things.

"Well, I'm damned!" said he in a low voice, and led the way.

I supposed my Hermes, as he led me to the lower regions, had had a little grog, but I said nothing, and followed him. 105 was on the port side, well aft. There was nothing remarkable about the state-room. The lower berth, like most of those upon the Kamtschatka, was double. There was plenty of room; there was the usual washing apparatus, calculated to convey an idea of luxury to the mind of a North American Indian; there were the usual inefficient racks of brown wood, in which it is more easy to hang a large-sized umbrella than the common tooth-brush of commerce. Upon the uninviting mattresses were carefully folded together those blankets which a

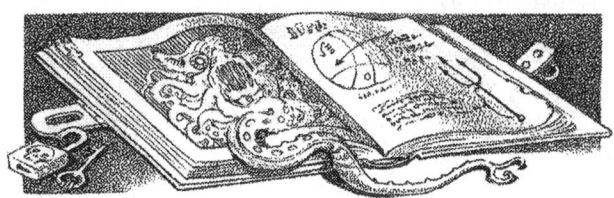

great modern humorist has aptly compared to cold buckwheat cakes. The question of towels was left entirely to the imagination. The glass decanters were filled with a transparent liquid faintly tinged with brown, but from which an odour less faint, but not more pleasing, ascended to the nostrils, like a far-off sea-sick reminiscence of oily machinery. Sad-coloured curtains half-closed the upper berth. The hazy June daylight shed a faint illumination upon the desolate little scene. Ugh! how I hate that state-room!

The steward deposited my traps and looked at me, as though he wanted to get away — probably in search of more passengers and more fees. It is always a good plan to start in favour with those functionaries, and I accordingly gave him certain coins there and then.

"I'll try and make yer comfortable all I can," he remarked, as he put the coins in his pocket. Nevertheless, there was a doubtful intonation in his voice which surprised me. Possibly his scale of fees had gone up, and he was not satisfied; but on the whole I was inclined to think that, as he himself would have expressed it, he was "the better for a glass". I was wrong, however, and did the man injustice.

II

Nothing especially worthy of mention occurred during that day. We left the pier punctually, and it was very pleasant to be fairly under way, for the weather was warm and sultry, and the motion of the steamer produced a refreshing breeze. Everybody knows what the first day at sea is like. People pace the decks and stare at each other, and occasionally meet acquaintances whom they did not know to be on board. There is the usual uncertainty as to whether the food will be good, bad, or indifferent, until the first two meals have put the matter beyond a doubt; there is the usual uncertainty about the weather, until the ship is fairly off Fire Island. The tables are crowded at first, and then suddenly thinned. Pale-faced people spring from their seats and precipitate themselves towards the door, and each old sailor breathes more freely as his sea-sick neighbour rushes from his side, leaving him plenty of elbow-room and an unlimited command over the mustard.

One passage across the Atlantic is very much like another, and we who cross very often do not make the voyage for the sake of novelty. Whales and icebergs are indeed always objects of interest, but, after all, one whale is very much like another whale, and one rarely sees an iceberg at close quarters. To the majority of us the most delightful moment of the day on board an ocean steamer is when we have taken our last turn on deck, have smoked our last cigar, and having succeeded in tiring ourselves, feel at liberty to turn in with a clear conscience. On that first night of the voyage I felt particularly lazy, and went to bed in 105 rather earlier than I usually do. As I turned in, I was amazed to see that I was to have a companion. A portmanteau, very like my own, lay in the opposite corner, and in the upper berth had been deposited a neatly folded rug, with a stick and umbrella. I had hoped to be alone, and I was disappointed; but I wondered who my room-mate was to be, and I determined to have a look at him.

Before I had been long in bed he entered. He was, as far as I could see, a very tall man, very thin, very pale, with sandy hair and whiskers and colourless grey eyes. He had about him, I thought, an air of rather dubious fashion; the sort of man you might see in Wall Street, without being able precisely to say what he was doing there — the sort of man who frequents the Café Anglais, who always seems to be alone and who drinks champagne; you might meet him on a racecourse, but he would never appear to be doing anything there either. A little over-dressed — a little odd. There are three or four of his kind on every ocean steamer. I made up my mind that I did not care to make his acquaintance, and I went to sleep saying to myself that I would study his habits in order to avoid him. If he rose early, I would rise late; if he went to bed late, I would go to bed early. I did not care to know him. If you once know people of that kind they are always turning up. Poor fellow! I need not have taken the trouble to come to so many decisions about him, for I never saw him again after that first night in 105.

I was sleeping soundly when I was suddenly waked by a loud noise. To judge from the sound, my room-mate must have sprung with a single leap from the upper berth to the floor. I heard him fumbling with the latch and bolt of the door, which opened almost immediately, and then I heard his footsteps as he ran at full speed down the passage, leaving the door open behind him. The ship was rolling a little, and I expected to hear him stumble or fall, but he ran as though he were running for his life. The door swung on its hinges with the motion of the vessel, and the sound annoyed me. I got up and shut it, and groped my way back to my berth in the darkness. I went to sleep again; but I have no idea how long I slept.

When I awoke it was still quite dark, but I felt a disagreeable sensation of cold, and it seemed to me that the air was damp. You know the peculiar smell of a cabin which has been wet with sea-water. I covered myself up as well as I could and dozed off again, framing complaints to be made the next day, and selecting the most powerful epithets in the language. I could hear my room-mate turn over in the upper berth. He had probably returned while I was asleep. Once I thought I heard him groan, and I argued that he was sea-sick. That is particularly unpleasant when one is below. Nevertheless I dozed off and slept till early daylight.

The ship was rolling heavily, much more than on the previous evening, and the grey light which came in through the porthole changed in tint with every movement according as the angle of the vessel's side turned the glass seawards or skywards. It was very cold — unaccountably so for the month of June. I turned my head and looked at the porthole, and saw to my surprise that it was wide open and hooked back. I believe I swore audibly. Then I got up and shut it. As I turned back I glanced at the upper berth. The curtains were drawn close together; my companion had probably felt cold as well as I. It struck me that I had slept enough. The state-room was uncomfortable, though, strange to say, I could not smell the dampness which had annoyed me in the night. My room-mate was still asleep — excellent opportunity for avoiding him, so I dressed at once and went on deck. The day was warm and cloudy, with an oily smell on the water. It was seven o'clock as I came out — much later than I had imagined. I came across the doctor, who was taking his first sniff of the morning air. He was a young man from the West of Ireland — a tremendous fellow, with black hair and blue eyes, already inclined to be stout; he had a happy-go-lucky, healthy look about him which was rather attractive.

"Fine morning," I said, by way of introduction.

"Well," said he, eyeing me with an air of ready interest, "it's a fine morning and it's not a fine morning. I don't think it's much of a morning."

"Well, no — it is not so very fine," said I.

"It's just what I call fuggly weather," said the doctor.

"It was very cold last night, I thought," I remarked. "However, when I looked about, I found that the porthole was wide open. I had not noticed it when I went to bed. And the state-room was damp, too."

"Damp!" said he. "Whereabouts are you?"

"One hundred and five —"

To my surprise the doctor started visibly, and stared at me.

"What is the matter?" I asked.

"Oh — nothing," he answered; "only everybody has complained of that state-room for the last three trips."

"I shall complain too," I said. "It has certainly not been properly aired. It is a shame!"

"I don't believe it can be helped," answered the doctor. "I believe there is something — well, it is not my business to frighten passengers."

"You need not be afraid of frightening me," I replied. "I can stand any amount of damp. If I should get a bad cold I will come to you."

I offered the doctor a cigar, which he took and examined very critically.

"It is not so much the damp," he remarked. "However, I dare say you will get on very well. Have you a room-mate?"

"Yes; a deuce of a fellow, who bolts out in the middle of the night, and leaves the door open."

Again the doctor glanced curiously at me. Then he lit the cigar and looked grave.

"Did he come back?" he asked presently.

"Yes. I was asleep, but I waked up, and heard him moving. Then I felt cold and went to sleep again. This morning I found the porthole open."

"Look here," said the doctor quietly, "I don't care much for this ship. I don't care a rap for her reputation. I tell you what I will do. I have a good-sized place up here. I will share it with you, though I don't know you from Adam."

I was very much surprised at the proposition. I could not imagine why he should take such a sudden interest in my welfare. However, his manner as he spoke of the ship was peculiar.

"You are very good, doctor," I said. "But, really, I believe even now the cabin could be aired, or cleaned out, or something. Why do you not care for the ship?"

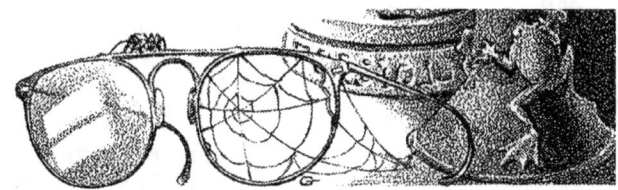

"We are not superstitious in our profession, sir," replied the doctor, "but the sea makes people so. I don't want to prejudice you, and I don't want to frighten you, but if you will take my advice you will move in here. I would as soon see you overboard," he added earnestly, "as know that you or any other man was to sleep in 105."

"Good gracious! Why?" I asked.

"Just because on the last three trips the people who have slept there actually have gone overboard," he answered gravely.

The intelligence was startling and exceedingly unpleasant, I confess. I looked hard at the doctor to see whether he was making game of me, but he looked perfectly serious. I thanked him warmly for his offer, but told him I intended to be the exception to the rule by which every one who slept in that particular state-room went overboard. He did not say much, but looked as grave as ever, and hinted that, before we got across, I should probably reconsider his proposal. In the course of time we went to breakfast, at which only an inconsiderable number of passengers assembled. I noticed that one or two of the officers who breakfasted with us looked grave. After breakfast I went into my state-room in order to get a book. The curtains of the upper berth were still closely drawn. Not a word was to be heard. My room-mate was probably still asleep.

As I came out I met the steward whose business it was to look after me. He whispered that the captain wanted to see me, and then scuttled away down the passage as if very anxious to avoid any questions. I went toward the captain's cabin, and found him waiting for me.

"Sir," said he, "I want to ask a favour of you."

I answered that I would do anything to oblige him.

"Your room-mate has disappeared," he said. "He is known to have turned in early last night. Did you notice anything extraordinary in his manner?"

The question coming, as it did, in exact confirmation of the fears the doctor had expressed half an hour earlier, staggered me.

"You don't mean to say he has gone overboard?" I asked.

"I fear he has," answered the captain.

"This is the most extraordinary thing —" I began.

"Why?" he asked.

"He is the fourth, then!" I exclaimed. In answer to another question from the captain, I explained, without mentioning the doctor, that I had heard the story concerning 105. He seemed very much annoyed at hearing that I knew of it. I told him what had occurred in the night.

"What you say," he replied, "coincides almost exactly with what was told me by the room-mates of two of the other three. They bolt out of bed and run down the passage. Two of them were seen to go overboard by the watch; we stopped and lowered boats, but they were not found. Nobody, however, saw or heard the man who was lost last night — if he is really lost. The steward, who is a superstitious fellow, perhaps, and expected something to go wrong, went to look for him, this morning, and found his berth empty, but his clothes lying about, just as he had left them. The steward was the only man on board who knew him by sight, and he has been searching everywhere for him. He has disappeared! Now, sir, I want to beg you not to mention the circumstance to any of the passengers; I don't want the ship to get a bad name, and nothing hangs about an ocean-goer like stories of suicides. You shall have your choice of any one of the officers' cabins you like, including my own, for the rest of the passage. Is that a fair bargain?"

"Very," said I; "and I am much obliged to you. But since I am alone, and have the state-room to myself, I would rather not move. If the steward will take out that unfortunate man's things, I would as lief stay where I am. I will not say anything about the matter, and I think I can promise you that I will not follow my room-mate."

The captain tried to dissuade me from my intention, but I preferred having a state-room alone to being the chum of any officer on board. I do not know whether I acted foolishly, but if I had taken his advice I should have had nothing more to tell. There would have remained the disagreeable coincidence of several suicides occurring among men who had slept in the same cabin, but that would have been all.

That was not the end of the matter, however, by any means. I obstinately made up my mind that I would not be disturbed by such tales, and I even went so far as to argue the question with the captain. There was something wrong about the state-room, I said. It was rather damp. The porthole had been left open last night. My room-mate might have been ill when he came on board, and he might have become delirious after he went to bed. He might even now be hiding somewhere on board, and might be found later. The place ought to be aired and the fastening of the port looked to. If the captain would give me leave, I would see that what I thought necessary were done immediately.

"Of course you have a right to stay where you are if you please," he replied, rather petulantly; "but I wish you would turn out and let me lock the place up, and be done with it."

I did not see it in the same light, and left the captain, after promising to be silent concerning the disappearance of my companion. The latter had had no acquaintances on board, and was not missed in the course of the day. Towards evening I met the doctor again, and he asked me whether I had changed my mind. I told him I had not.

"Then you will before long," he said, very gravely.

III

We played whist in the evening, and I went to bed late. I will confess now that I felt a disagreeable sensation when I entered my state-room. I could not help thinking of the tall man I had seen on the previous night, who was now dead, drowned, tossing about in the long swell, two or three hundred miles astern. His face rose very distinctly before me as I undressed, and I even went so far as to draw back the curtains of the upper berth, as though to persuade myself that he was actually gone. I also bolted the door of the state-room. Suddenly I became aware that the porthole was open, and fastened back. This was more than I could stand. I hastily threw on my dressing-gown and went in search of Robert, the steward of my passage. I was very angry, I remember, and when I found him I dragged him roughly to the door of 105, and pushed him towards the open porthole.

"What the deuce do you mean, you scoundrel, by leaving that port open every night? Don't you know it is against the regulations? Don't you know that if the ship heeled and the water began to come in, ten men could not shut it? I will report you to the captain, you blackguard, for endangering the ship!"

I was exceedingly wroth. The man trembled and turned pale, and then began to shut the round glass plate with the heavy brass fittings.

"Why don't you answer me?" I said roughly.

"If you please, sir," faltered Robert, "there's nobody on board as can keep this 'ere port shut at night. You can try it yourself, sir. I ain't a-going to

stop hany longer on board o' this vessel, sir; I ain't, indeed. But if I was you, sir, I'd just clear out and go and sleep with the surgeon, or something, I would. Look 'ere, sir, is that fastened what you may call securely, or not, sir? Try it, sir, see if it will move a hinch."

I tried the port, and found it perfectly tight.

"Well, sir," continued Robert triumphantly, "I wager my reputation as a A1 steward that in 'arf an hour it will be open again; fastened back, too, sir, that's the horful thing — fastened back!"

I examined the great screw and the looped nut that ran on it.

"If I find it open in the night, Robert, I will give you a sovereign. It is not possible. You may go."

"Soverin' did you say, sir? Very good, sir. Thank ye, sir. Good-night, sir. Pleasant reepose, sir, and all manner of hinchantin' dreams, sir."

Robert scuttled away, delighted at being released. Of course, I thought he was trying to account for his negligence by a silly story, intended to frighten me, and I disbelieved him. The consequence was that he got his sovereign, and I spent a very peculiarly unpleasant night.

I went to bed, and five minutes after I had rolled myself up in my blankets the inexorable Robert extinguished the light that burned steadily behind the ground-glass pane near the door. I lay quite still in the dark trying to go to sleep, but I soon found that impossible. It had been some satisfaction to be angry with the steward, and the diversion had banished that unpleasant sensation I had at first experienced when I thought of the drowned man who had been my chum; but I was no longer sleepy, and I lay awake for some time, occasionally glancing at the porthole, which I could just see from where I lay, and which, in the darkness, looked like a faintly-luminous soup-plate suspended in blackness. I believe I must have lain there for an hour, and, as I remember, I was just dozing into sleep when I was roused by a draught of cold air, and by distinctly feeling the spray of the sea blown upon my face. I started to my feet, and not having allowed in the dark for the motion of the ship, I was instantly thrown violently across the state-room upon the couch which

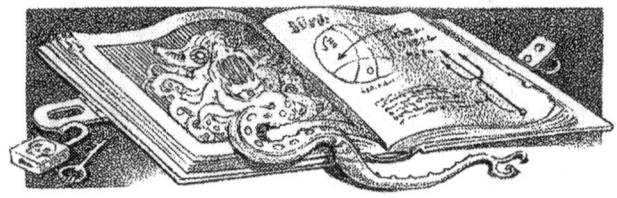

was placed beneath the port-hole. I recovered myself immediately, however, and climbed upon my knees. The porthole was again wide open and fastened back!

Now these things are facts. I was wide awake when I got up, and I should certainly have been waked by the fall had I still been dozing. Moreover, I bruised my elbows and knees badly, and the bruises were there on the following morning to testify to the fact, if I myself had doubted it. The porthole was wide open and fastened back — a thing so unaccountable that I remember very well feeling astonishment rather than fear when I discovered it. I at once closed the plate again, and screwed down the loop nut with all my strength. It was very dark in the state-room. I reflected that the port had certainly been opened within an hour after Robert had at first shut it in my presence, and I determined to watch it, and see whether it would open again. Those brass fittings are very heavy and by no means easy to move; I could not believe that the clump had been turned by the shaking of the screw. I stood peering out through the thick glass at the alternate white and grey streaks of the sea that foamed beneath the ship's side. I must have remained there a quarter of an hour.

Suddenly, as I stood, I distinctly heard something moving behind me in one of the berths, and a moment afterwards, just as I turned instinctively to look — though I could, of course, see nothing in the darkness — I heard a very faint groan. I sprang across the state-room, and tore the curtains of the upper berth aside, thrusting in my hands to discover if there were any one there. There was some one.

I remember that the sensation as I put my hands forward was as though I were plunging them into the air of a damp cellar, and from behind the curtains came a gust of wind that smelled horribly of stagnant sea-water. I laid hold of something that had the shape of a man's arm, but was smooth, and wet, and icy cold. But suddenly, as I pulled, the creature sprang violently forward against me, a clammy oozy mass, as it seemed to me, heavy and wet, yet endowed with a sort of supernatural strength. I reeled across the state-room, and in an instant the door opened and the thing rushed out. I had not had time to be frightened, and quickly recovering myself, I sprang through the door and gave chase at the top of my speed, but I was too late. Ten yards before me I could see — I am sure I saw it — a dark shadow moving in the dimly lighted passage, quickly as the shadow of a fast horse thrown before a dog-cart by the lamp on a dark night. But in a moment it had disappeared, and I found myself holding on to the polished rail that ran along the bulkhead where the passage turned towards the companion. My hair stood on end, and the cold perspiration rolled down my face. I am not ashamed of it in the least: I was very badly frightened.

Still I doubted my senses, and pulled myself together. It was absurd, I thought. The Welsh rare-bit I had eaten had disagreed with me. I had been in a nightmare. I made my way back to my state-room, and entered it with an effort. The whole place smelled of stagnant sea-water, as it had when I had waked on the previous evening. It required my utmost strength to go in, and grope among my things for a box of wax lights. As I lighted a railway reading lantern which I always carry in case I want to read after the lamps are out, I perceived that the porthole was again open, and a sort of creeping horror began to take possession of me which I never felt before, nor wish to feel again. But I got a light and proceeded to examine the upper berth, expecting to find it drenched with sea-water.

But I was disappointed. The bed had been slept in, and the smell of the sea was strong; but the bedding was as dry as a bone. I fancied that Robert had not had the courage to make the bed after the accident of the previous night — it had all been a hideous dream. I drew the curtains back as far as I could and examined the place very carefully. It was perfectly dry. But the porthole was open again. With a sort of dull bewilderment of horror I closed it and screwed it down, and thrusting my heavy stick through the brass loop, wrenched it with all my might, till the thick metal began to bend under the pressure. Then I hooked my reading lantern into the red velvet at the head of the couch, and sat down to recover my senses if I could. I sat there all night, unable to think of rest — hardly able to think at all. But the porthole remained closed, and I did not believe it would now open again without the application of a considerable force.

The morning dawned at last, and I dressed myself slowly, thinking over all that had happened in the night. It was a beautiful day and I went on deck, glad to get out into the early, pure sunshine, and to smell the breeze from the blue water, so different from the noisome, stagnant odour of my state-room. Instinctively I turned aft, towards the surgeon's cabin. There he stood, with a pipe in his mouth, taking his morning airing precisely as on the preceding day.

"Good-morning," said he quietly, but looking at me with evident curiosity.

"Doctor, you were quite right," said I. "There is something wrong about that place."

"I thought you would change your mind," he answered, rather triumphantly. "You have had a bad night, eh? Shall I make you a pick-me-up? I have a capital recipe."

"No, thanks," I cried. "But I would like to tell you what happened."

I then tried to explain as clearly as possible precisely what had occurred, not omitting to state that I had been scared as I had never been scared in my whole life before. I dwelt particularly on the phenomenon of the porthole, which was a fact to which I could testify, even if the rest had been an illusion. I had closed it twice in the night, and the second time I had actually bent the brass in wrenching it with my stick. I believe I insisted a good deal on this point.

"You seem to think I am likely to doubt the story," said the doctor, smiling at the detailed account of the state of the porthole. "I do not doubt it in the least. I renew my invitation to you. Bring your traps here, and take half my cabin."

"Come and take half of mine for one night," I said. "Help me to get at the bottom of this thing."

"You will get to the bottom of something else if you try," answered the doctor.

"What?" I asked.

"The bottom of the sea. I am going to leave this ship. It is not canny."

"Then you will not help me to find out —"

"Not I," said the doctor quickly. "It is my business to keep my wits about me — not to go fiddling about with ghosts and things."

"Do you really believe it is a ghost?" I enquired, rather contemptuously. But as I spoke I remembered very well the horrible sensation of the supernatural which had got possession of me during the night. The doctor turned sharply on me —

"Have you any reasonable explanation of these things to offer?" he asked. "No; you have not. Well, you say you will find an explanation. I say that you won't, sir, simply because there is not any."

"But, my dear sir," I retorted, "do you, a man of science, mean to tell me that such things cannot be explained?"

"I do," he answered stoutly. "And, if they could,

I would not be concerned in the explanation."

I did not care to spend another night alone in the state-room, and yet I was obstinately determined to get at the root of the disturbances. I do not believe there are many men who would have slept there alone, after passing two such nights. But I made up my mind to try it, if I could not get any one to share a watch with me. The doctor was evidently not inclined for such an experiment. He said he was a surgeon, and that in case any accident occurred on board he must be always in readiness. He could not afford to have his nerves unsettled. Perhaps he was quite right, but I am inclined to think that his precaution was prompted by his inclination. On enquiry, he informed me that there was no one on board who would be likely to join me in my investigations, and after a little more conversation I left him. A little later I met the captain, and told him my story. I said that, if no one would spend the night with me, I would ask leave to have the light burning all night, and would try it alone.

"Look here," said he, "I will tell you what I will do. I will share your watch myself, and we will see what happens. It is my belief that we can find out between us. There may be some fellow skulking on board, who steals a passage by frightening the passengers. It is just possible that there may be something odd in the carpentering of that berth."

I suggested taking the ship's carpenter below and examining the place; but I was overjoyed at the captain's offer to spend the night with me. He accordingly sent for the workman and ordered him to do anything I required. We went below at once. I had all the bedding cleared out of the upper berth, and we examined the place thoroughly to see if there was a board loose anywhere, or a panel which could be opened or pushed aside. We tried the planks everywhere, tapped the flooring, unscrewed the fittings of the lower berth and took it to pieces — in short, there was not a square inch of the state-room which was not searched and tested. Everything was in perfect order, and we put everything back in its place. As we were finishing our work, Robert came to the door and looked in.

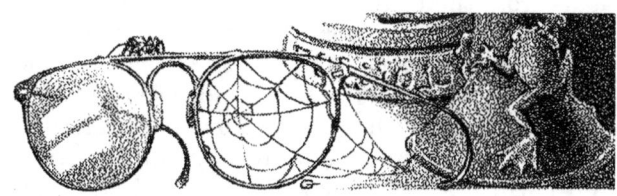

"Well, sir — find anything, sir?" he asked, with a ghastly grin.

"You were right about the porthole, Robert," I said, and I gave him the promised sovereign. The carpenter did his work silently and skilfully, following my directions. When he had done he spoke.

"I'm a plain man, sir," he said. "But it's my belief you had better just turn out your things, and let me run half a dozen four-inch screws through the door of this cabin. There's no good never came o' this cabin yet, sir, and that's all about it. There's been four lives lost out o' here to my own remembrance, and that in four trips. Better give it up, sir — better give it up!"

"I will try it for one night more," I said.

"Better give it up, sir — better give it up! It's a precious bad job," repeated the workman, putting his tools in his bag and leaving the cabin.

But my spirits had risen considerably at the prospect of having the captain's company, and I made up my mind not to be prevented from going to the end of the strange business. I abstained from Welsh rare-bits and grog that evening, and did not even join in the customary game of whist. I wanted to be quite sure of my nerves, and my vanity made me anxious to make a good figure in the captain's eyes.

IV

The captain was one of those splendidly tough and cheerful specimens of seafaring humanity whose combined courage, hardihood, and calmness in difficulty leads them naturally into high positions of trust. He was not the man to be led away by an idle tale, and the mere fact that he was willing to join me in the investigation was proof that he thought there was something seriously wrong, which could not be accounted for on ordinary theories, nor laughed down as a common superstition. To some extent, too, his reputation was at stake, as well as the reputation of the ship. It is no light thing to lose passengers overboard, and he knew it.

About ten o'clock that evening, as I was smoking a last cigar, he came up to me, and drew me aside from the beat of the other passengers who were patrolling the deck in the warm darkness.

"This is a serious matter, Mr. Brisbane," he said. "We must make up our minds either way — to be disappointed or to have a pretty rough time of it. You see I cannot afford to laugh at the affair, and I will ask you to sign your name to a state-ment of whatever occurs. If nothing happens tonight we will try it again tomorrow and next day. Are you ready?"

So we went below, and entered the state-room. As we went in I could see Robert the steward, who stood a little further down the passage, watching us, with his usual grin, as though certain that something dreadful was about to happen. The captain closed the door behind us and bolted it.

"Supposing we put your portmanteau before the door," he suggested. "One of us can sit on it. Nothing can get out then. Is the port screwed down?"

I found it as I had left it in the morning. Indeed, without using a lever, as I had done, no one could have opened it. I drew back the curtains of the upper berth so that I could see well into it. By the captain's advice I lighted my reading lantern, and placed it so that it shone upon the white sheets above. He insisted upon sitting on the portmanteau, declaring that he wished to be able to swear that he had sat before the door.

Then he requested me to search the state-room thoroughly, an operation very soon accomplished, as it consisted merely in looking beneath the lower berth and under the couch below the porthole. The spaces were quite empty.

"It is impossible for any human being to get in," I said, "or for any human being to open the port."

"Very good," said the captain calmly. "If we see anything now, it must be either imagination or something supernatural."

I sat down on the edge of the lower berth.

"The first time it happened," said the captain, crossing his legs and leaning back against the door, "was in March. The passenger who slept here, in the upper berth, turned out have been a lunatic — at all events, he was known to have been a little touched, and he had taken his passage without the knowledge of his friends. He rushed out in the middle of the night, and threw himself overboard, before the officer who had the watch could stop him. We stopped and lowered a boat; it was a quiet night, just before that heavy weather came on; but we could not find him. Of course his suicide was afterwards accounted for on the ground of his insanity."

"I suppose that often happens?" I remarked, rather absently.

"Not often — no," said the captain; "never before in my experience, though I have heard of it happening on board of other ships. Well, as I was saying, that occurred in March. On the very next trip — What are you looking at?" he asked, stopping suddenly in his narration.

I believe I gave no answer. My eyes were riveted upon the porthole. It seemed to me that the brass loop-nut was beginning to turn very slowly upon the screw — so slowly, however, that I was not sure it moved at all. I watched it intently, fixing its position in my mind, and trying to ascertain whether it changed. Seeing where I was looking, the captain looked too.

"It moves!" he exclaimed, in a tone of conviction. "No, it does not," he added, after a minute.

"If it were the jarring of the screw," said I, "it would have opened during the day; but I found it this evening jammed tight as I left it this morning."

I rose and tried the nut. It was certainly loosened, for by an effort I could move it with my hands.

"The strange thing," said the captain, "is that the second man who was lost is supposed to have got through that very port. We had a terrible time over it. It was in the middle of the night, and the weather was very heavy; there was an alarm that one of the ports was open and the sea running in. I came below and found everything flooded, the water pouring in every time she rolled, and the whole port swinging from the top bolts — not the porthole in the middle. Well, we managed to shut it, but the water did some damage. Ever since that the place smells of sea-water from time to time. We supposed the passenger had thrown himself out, though the Lord only knows how he did it. The steward kept telling me that he cannot keep anything shut here. Upon my word — I can smell it now, cannot you?" he enquired, sniffing the air suspiciously.

"Yes — distinctly," I said, and I shuddered as that same odour of stagnant sea-water grew stronger in the cabin. "Now, to smell like this, the place must be damp," I continued, "and yet when I examined it with the carpenter this morning everything was perfectly dry. It is most extraordinary — hallo!"

My reading lantern, which had been placed in the upper berth, was suddenly extinguished. There was still a good deal of light from the pane of ground glass near the door, behind which loomed the regulation lamp. The ship rolled heavily, and the curtain of the upper berth swung far out into the state-room and back again. I rose quickly from my seat on the edge of the bed, and the captain at the same moment started to his feet with a loud cry of surprise. I had turned with the intention of taking down the lantern to examine it, when I heard his exclamation, and immediately afterwards his call for help. I sprang towards him. He was wrestling with all his might with the brass loop of the port. It seemed to turn against his hands in spite of all his efforts. I caught up my cane, a heavy oak stick I always used to carry, and thrust it through the ring and bore on it with all my strength. But the strong wood snapped suddenly and I fell upon the couch. When I rose again the port was wide open, and the captain was standing with his back against the door, pale to the lips.

"There is something in that berth!" he cried, in a strange voice, his eyes almost starting from his head. "Hold the door, while I look — it shall not escape us, whatever it is!"

But instead of taking his place, I sprang upon the lower bed, and seized something which lay in the upper berth.

It was something ghostly, horrible beyond words, and it moved in my grip. It was like the body of a man long drowned, and yet it moved, and had the strength of ten men living; but I gripped it with all my might — the slippery, oozy, horrible thing — the dead white eyes seemed to stare at me out of the dusk; the putrid odour of rank sea-water was about it, and its shiny hair hung in foul wet curls over its dead face. I wrestled with the dead thing; it thrust itself upon me and forced me back and nearly broke my arms; it wound its corpse's arms about my neck, the living death, and overpowered me, so that I, at last, cried aloud and fell, and left my hold.

As I fell the thing sprang across me, and seemed to throw itself upon the captain. When I last saw him on his feet his face was white and his lips set. It seemed to me that he struck a violent blow at the dead being, and then he, too, fell forward upon his face, with an inarticulate cry of horror.

The thing paused an instant, seeming to hover over his prostrate body, and I could have screamed again for very fright, but I had no voice left. The thing vanished suddenly, and it seemed to my disturbed senses that it made its exit

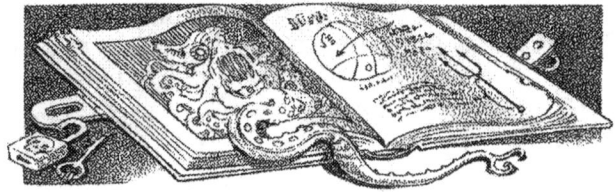

through the open port, though how that was possible, considering the smallness of the aperture, is more than any one can tell. I lay a long time upon the floor, and the captain lay beside me. At last I partially recovered my senses and moved, and instantly I knew that my arm was broken — the small bone of the left forearm near the wrist.

I got upon my feet somehow, and with my remaining hand I tried to raise the captain. He groaned and moved, and at last came to himself. He was not hurt, but he seemed badly stunned.

Well, do you want to hear any more? There is nothing more.

That is the end of my story. The carpenter carried out his scheme of running half a dozen four-inch screws through the door of 105; and if ever you take a passage in the Kamtschatka, you may ask for a berth in that state-room. You will be told that it is engaged — yes — it is engaged by that dead thing.

I finished the trip in the surgeon's cabin. He doctored my broken arm, and advised me not to "fiddle about with ghosts and things" any more.

The captain was very silent, and never sailed again in that ship, though it is still running. And I will not sail in her either. It was a very disagreeable experience, and I was very badly frightened, which is a thing I do not like. That is all. That is how I saw a ghost — if it was a ghost. It was dead, anyhow.   Ω

Francis Marion Crawford (1854–1909) was a best-selling novelist in his day, noted for his well-crafted and accurately-researched romances set in Italy and India. He is best remembered today for his posthumous supernatural collection *Wandering Ghosts* (1911) from which this story is taken.

No less an authority than H.P. Lovecraft pronounced "The Upper Berth" one of the finest of all horror stories. Other notable works from the same collection include "The Screaming Skull" and "For Blood is the Life," an early vampire story. His novels *The Witch of Prague* (1891) and *Khaled* (1891) are also of interest. They remain in print from Wildside Press. The present story has appeared in *Weird Tales* once before, in the June 1926 issue.

I HAVE NEVER . . .

I have never heard sweet calypso sung at sunset
  When steel waxed hot under the drummers' hands,
    Iron ping-pong rhythms wringing passion from desolate souls.
But I have stalked calypso drummers in the Trinidadian night
  When drunk on rum or weed they wove across traffic-choked streets,
    And met my fangs in back ways no cry could escape.

I have never seen Ipanema Beach at two in the afternoon
  When young men and women strutted in thong swimsuits,
    Their browning curves swelling wet under glowing beams.
But I have glided over the sands of Ipanema in the dark
  When young lovers and bums spent their juices on the moonstruck grains,
    And died with despair in their hollow eyes.

I have never smelled Spanish moss from a Mississippi oak at noon
  When gumbo boiled and bourbon rolled down sensuous throats
    Of proud, seasoned men and women whose eyes dance in shadows.
But I have smelled the blood of those who have known the world
  When they tasted that last knowledge of chaos and gloom,
    Their haughty ways dwindling down to clay as I drank their lives away.

— **Paul Crumrine**

WILDSIDE PULP CLASSICS: PULP FACSIMILE SERIES
Series editor: John Gregory Betancourt

#1: *Spicy Mystery Stories* (August 1935)

Includes Robert Leslie Bellem, Atwater Culpepper, Ellery Watson Calder, Carl Moore, E. Hoffman Price, Arthur Wallace, and more.

#2: *Ghost Stories* (June 1931)

Stories by Conrad Richter (best known as the author of The Light in the Forest*) and E. & H. Heron featuring psychic detective, Flaxman Low.*

#3: *Spicy Mystery Stories* (February 1937)

The Feb 1937 issue features Robert Leslie Bellem, Lew Merrill (Victor Rousseau) Hugh Speer, Justin Case (Hugh B. Cave), & many others!

#4: *Strange Tales* #7 (January 1933)

This issue features Hugh B. Cave's classic "Murgunstrumm," as well as stories by Robert E. Howard, Henry S. Whitehead, and many more.

#5: *The Black Mask* #2 (May 1920)

2nd issue of classic mystery mag, where hardboiled noir fiction was born!

#6: *Tales of Magic and Mystery* (February 1928)

Legendary rare early fantasy magazine!

#7: *The Phantom Detective* #1 (February 1933)

The premiere issue of the detective-hero pulp!

#8: *Submarine Stories* (March 1930)

Rare pulp magazine, featuring stories and articles about (what else?) subs!

#9: *Sinister Stories* #1 (Feb 1940)

The first issue of this "weird menace" pulp!

#10: *The Thrill Book* (Sept. 1, 1919)

Facsimile reprint of a legendary magazine, one of the holy grails of pulp collecting!

- -

Yes! Please send me the following books, for which I enclose payment. (Or order online with a credit card at www.wildsidepress.com, or through your favorite online bookseller.)

☐ *Spicy Mystery Stories* (Aug.1935) - $19.95
☐ *Ghost Stories* (June 1931) - $19.95
☐ *Spicy Mystery Stories* (Feb. 1937) - $19.95
☐ *Strange Tales* #7 (January 1933) - $15.00
☐ *The Black Mask* #2 (January 1920) - $19.95
☐ *Tales of Magic and Mystery* (Feb. 1928) - $19.95
☐ *The Phantom Detective* #1 (Feb. 1933) - $19.95
☐ *Submarine Stories* (March. 1930) - $19.95
☐ *Sinister Stories* (Feb 1940) - $19.95
☐ *The Thrill Book* (Feb 1940) - $19.95

Mail to: Wildside Press
P.O. Box 301
Holicong, PA 18928-0301.

U.S. shipping: $3.95 for 1-2 books, $1 per additional book.
Shipping to other countries: please see web site:
www.wildsidepress.com

Name: _____

Address:_____

Address:_____

www.ingramcontent.com/pod-product-compliance
Lightning Source LLC
Chambersburg PA
CBHW081148170626
46809CB00010B/3140